Cinder and Ella

Cinder and Ella

Melissa Lemon

Sweetwater Books
An imprint of Cedar Fort, Inc.
Springville, Utah

This is a work of fiction. The characters, names, incidents, places, and dialogue are products of the author's imagination, and are not to be construed as real.

ISBN 13: 978-1-59955-906-3

Published by Sweetwater Books, an imprint of Cedar Fort, Inc.
2373 W. 700 S., Springville, UT 84663
Distributed by Cedar Fort, Inc., www.cedarfort.com

LIBRARY OF CONGRESS CATALOGING-IN-PUBLICATION DATA

Lemon, Melissa, 1980- author.
Cinder and Ella / Melissa Lemon.
pages cm
ISBN 978-1-59955-906-3
1. Cinderella (Legendary character)--Fiction. 2. Cinderella (Tale)--Adaptations. I. Title.

PS3612.E473C56 2011
813'.6--dc23

2011026682

Cover design by Brian Halley
Cover design © 2011 by Lyle Mortimer
Edited and typeset by Heidi Doxey

Printed in the United States of America

10 9 8 7 6 5 4 3 2 1

Printed on acid-free paper

For my daughters—follow your dreams.
And for Ryan, my best of everything.

Prologue

If you drink water and breathe air, then you have heard the story of Cinderella. And, if you drink water and breathe air, you have heard it . . . wrong.

There was no fairy godmother, no glass slipper. There was no wicked stepmother or wicked stepsisters. There wasn't even a prince, at least not in the way that you might think. And if you're expecting everyone to live happily ever after, you may end up being disappointed. But a happy ending isn't something that can be expected or predicted. And while it all happened long ago, the events that took place were memorable enough to stand the test of time, even if the details have been altered.

The true story of Cinderella is about a family that consisted of a father, a mother, and four sisters. Three of the sisters looked like their mother, with long, thick hair; dark eyes; and handsomely robust figures. Only the third daughter resembled her father. They were both thin and had honey-colored hair and hazel eyes. There were only three years between the first three daughters, and another five years to the youngest. The family lived in a small cottage on the side of a steep mountain. It was embedded deep in a grove of aspen trees and was many miles from any other structure in the kingdom.

For a time, the family was happy. The father and mother found joy in their daughters, played with them while they were still small, took the time to tuck them in at night, and treated them all as precious jewels. The sisters played well together and grew in friendship and love, with only the occasional sisterly squabble, like when the eldest would rip the youngest daughter's favorite toy from her hands merely to see her wail.

But, as we all know, happiness doesn't always last. As the sisters grew older, an evil came upon the kingdom. And while they did not know it, the prince, who had started the works of darkness, would change the fate of their entire lives.

Their troubles began with a knock on the door late one evening. The youngest, who was still a small child, was already sleeping, and the other girls had gone upstairs for the night as well.

The door was answered. It was the prince. His towering height and dark, handsome features could earn him entry into any house. Once inside a home, he could captivate an audience with his charm and pleasantness. And his smile alone was enough to make many women swoon over him.

He didn't stay long at the cottage of Willow Top that night, but in those few minutes, the prince was able to ignite something in the father. Prince Monticello spoke of the injustice and lunacy of the king. Most of the prince's words were pure deception, but Weston of Willow Top was trusting. He believed the prince, who was barely old enough to be considered a man. Even the mother, Adela, was lulled at first, but when she saw the changes that began to take place in her husband, she knew the prince was not out to help the kingdom.

After that night, the father could not get the prince's words out of his head. His voice, the things he had said, even his laughter continued to ring in the father's ears until he was bewitched by a dark, invisible spell. Weston was so overtaken with thoughts of evil and corruption that everything he spoke became bitterness and gloom. He began treating his wife and daughters poorly until he ignored them altogether. The small blacksmith shop he owned was neglected and closed. Eventually, he became little more than a shadow or a ghost, until one day, he disappeared, leaving his wife and daughters to wonder if he was even alive.

This process was so gradual that by the time Weston was gone, his three oldest daughters were practically grown.

The end result was havoc in place of happiness. Contention was now a constant guest in the house, and the occasional, small quarrels between the sisters turned to fits of rage. They would often say nasty things to each other, hurt each other, or simply not speak to one another for weeks at a time.

One day, one of the daughters was about to cut a cake for somebody's birthday. The oldest sister was relentlessly throwing a horrible tantrum because she wanted to cut the cake. So the third daughter grabbed a handful of the cake and smeared it into her older sister's hair. The eldest daughter slapped her hard across the face, and the third daughter ran to her room, her cheek stinging and red. After this, the mother announced that birthdays would no longer be celebrated in the house.

Another time, two of the sisters were fighting about to whom a certain dress really belonged, and by the end of it, they both had a bit of a bald spot. The mother took all of the dresses in the house away for a time so that they had to walk about in only their underclothes. This was quite embarrassing for the three eldest girls, who were well into blossoming.

Devastated by all of this—especially the disappearance of her husband, whom she loved dearly—the mother sat at an old spinning wheel day after day after day. She would spin yarn from early in the morning until well into the night. She scarcely ate and soon became as thin and weak as a young tree seedling. She slept so poorly that her eyes sunk into her head and her cheek bones became more defined. Her daughters were little more than pebbles on the side of the road to her, or so it seemed.

Now, it is true in all families that when one is suffering, every member of the family is made to suffer in their own way. The mother shut out most of the world and lived inside the walls of her own despair. She became much of a ghost herself, and her daughters were left without care.

The eldest daughter, Katrina, who had once been almost agreeable, became much like a beast you might meet in the forest. She was not the most beautiful of the sisters, but she was the tallest and most demanding, and perhaps that is why she got her way most of the time. She would go to the mother and cry for this or that.

"Mother, I need a new pair of shoes," she would say. "Mother, my hair needs brushing!" or "Mother, I must have a new dress or I will never come out of my room again."

Little did she realize that that would have been a reward to her mother and sisters. But the mother would take some of the yarn she was spinning and give it to her eldest daughter without any thought.

"Go, child. Go to the village and get yourself a pair of shoes."

"The village is too far away for me to walk!"

"Then have your sisters go and get them for you."

"Cinder!" she would cry at the top of her lungs. "Mother says you are to go to the village and get me some shoes!"

Cinder was the second oldest child and was so named because from the womb she had hair the color of ash. Cinder became the family servant, and for the most part, she bore it all well. She was the most beautiful of all the daughters, on the inside and out.

"I'll go in the morning, Katrina, dear."

Cinder had a natural calm temper and a desire to serve others. She didn't mind taking over the responsibilities of her father and mother in caring for her sisters and could, for the most part, avoid fighting with them. Even before the family had begun to spiral downward, the girl could be found going about the village closest to their home and taking some time to read to an elderly man or woman or to care for somebody's small child. She was loved by all who knew her.

Beatrice was the youngest child in the family. While she had the same dark hair and eyes as her mother, she was not as comely. Her hair was brittle, and her eyes were too small on her chubby face. Her suffering came in the form of being spoiled. That may sound strange, but Beatrice became so accustomed to having everything given to her that she was nearly helpless. Cinder dressed her, bathed her, and fed her. At the age of eleven, the child would not even buckle her own shoes. Beatrice was given something every time she opened her mouth.

"Mama . . ."

And her mother would place a morsel of bread into her mouth.

"Cinda . . ."

And Cinder would give her whatever she was pointing at.

"Katty . . ."

And Katrina would stick out her tongue and then give her some sweets to keep her from crying. Naturally, Beatrice became a large, disagreeable child. If she wanted anything, she merely had to open her mouth and it would be placed within the grasp of her hands . . . or teeth.

Beatrice learned quickly, however, not to ask for anything from the third daughter, who would simply smack her on her arm and say, "Go away and leave me alone, you little brat." It didn't matter much to Beatrice, since the others gave her everything she needed, everything she wanted, and even more still. But once in a while, Beatrice would run to her mother screaming that her sister had hit her or kicked her or thrown her out into the snow. Much of this was exaggerated; it would have been more accurate to say that she had looked at Beatrice from across the room. But in order to keep the young one from throwing a terrible fit, their mother would punish the third daughter, whose only likeness to her mother was the color of her eyebrows.

This third daughter, who had been closest to her father, took it all very hard. She hated to see her mother spinning away every hour of the day, hated to see her beloved Cinder turned into the family servant, and she hated that her other sisters became so intolerable. With nobody to care for her anymore, and having a natural ability to take care of herself, that is exactly what she did. Her name was Ella.

1

"Ella, will you walk with me to the village to get a pair of shoes for Katrina?" Cinder was gathering a few things for the walk, like a shawl in case it became cool in the shade of all the trees, and a cap, in case the sun was making its way through the leaves.

Ella was sitting on the bed that she, Cinder, and Beatrice shared (because Katrina insisted on having her own room and bed) and flipping through one of the few books the family owned, wishing she knew what the words on the pages said. "I think I'd rather crawl under the house and sweep all the dirt away." She glanced at Cinder for a reaction. The two had similar facial features, and had it not been for their physical differences everywhere else, anyone would have known they were sisters.

Cinder always gave Ella the benefit of the doubt, but Ella really did not care to give in to the ridiculous requests of her eldest and younger sisters.

"I would like to get out for a while, though. That noisy little Beatrice is driving me batty." Ella closed the book and tossed it onto the bed. "I'll walk with you through the wood and then wait for you at the edge of the village."

"Thank you, Ella. I don't know what I'd do without you."

It was half a day's journey to the village, and the girls walked quietly through all the fallen, crunching leaves of the years before. It was early summer, and the sunbeams were beginning to pierce their way through the limbs of all the trees. As they reached the village, Ella sat down on a large rock and Cinder continued on to the shoemaker's. A man, who had long been acquainted with the family, stopped when he saw Ella.

"Good day, Miss . . . uh . . ."

"It's Ella. Good day, sir," she said in her shy, quiet voice.

"I saw your lovely sister Cinder just now at the shoemaker's. She is such a darling girl. My children and wife absolutely adore her. And how are your mother and father?"

"They are well, sir. Thank you for asking."

"I have not seen them lately. I used to see your father every day on my way to the village. I'll never forget how he helped fix our house when the roof caved in after the great rain. You were probably still a baby."

"He has been working lately . . . on the other side of the mountain, sir. My mother has taken to much work also."

"Yes, your mother makes the finest yarn. Please give them my regard."

"I will. Good day, sir."

"Good day." The man walked down the path that led away from the village and vanished from sight.

Ella did not like to lie, but she would not express to anyone the difficulties that the family was facing. It had swallowed too much of her heart and was painful for her to talk about. She and Cinder were both too proud to ask for help anyway, and Cinder maintained hope that soon everything would be back to normal. Ella was not as sure. She could feel the evil in her house and around the kingdom, as if it were ever lurking just below the surface of some invisible veil. It had permeated her home, causing the current state of her family, and she could feel it crawling up her skin as she walked through the woods, the trees bending and groaning. It was apparent in the eyes of some men in the village, who would look upon her and her sisters as if they were prey.

Three other people stopped to talk to Ella while she waited. None of them could remember her name. They each inquired after Cinder and expressed to Ella what a wonderful girl she had for a sister. One woman even said that she hoped Cinder would someday marry one of her sons and become her daughter-in-law. Ella, of course, agreed with them regarding what a good person Cinder was, but she often felt as though she wasn't noticed, as though she was the texture of a blade of grass, or a twig by the side of the road, or the hair up one's nose that is never quite in view.

The girls returned home to quite a scene. Tears were pouring from Beatrice's eyes as she wailed. Katrina was looking into the mirror, seemingly unaware of the noise, and Mother was spinning.

"Where are my shoes?"

"They're here," Cinder said, holding them out to her sister on her way to Beatrice. She sat down by the child and tried to calm her.

"Cinder and Ella, where have you been? Your sisters have needed you."

"We went to the village, Mother . . . to get shoes for Katrina." Cinder tried to give Beatrice toys and food to calm her, but nothing soothed the child. Ella stood, watching angrily from the door as Beatrice repeatedly slapped away everything that Cinder tried to give her.

Katrina tried on her new shoes. "They're too small! I'll need another pair!"

"Cinder-n-Ella, you will have to go back tomorrow and get another pair for your sister. Please, take the child from me so that I can work." The exasperation in Adela's voice made Ella twitch, but she did not intervene.

Cinder picked up Beatrice with difficulty—the girl was not a small child anymore—taking several smacks in the process. She headed up the small staircase with the girl screaming and kicking in her arms. Ella followed.

"I won't go," Ella said after Beatrice fell asleep that night.

"You may stay if you would prefer, Ella. I can manage on my own. You are a good sister."

Ella watched Cinder stroke Beatrice's hair. Her sister's goodness was a constant sting in Ella's withering heart. She wished that she could be as sweet and kind. "I am not a good sister, Cinder. Not like you."

"Cinder-n-Ella!" Mother yelled from downstairs. "Katrina needs her hair brushed before she can go to bed."

"I'll go," Cinder said, as if she really needed to. Ella had no intention of laying a finger on Katrina's hair, no matter how soft and beautiful it was. Cinder kissed Ella on the forehead and went downstairs.

Ella looked out her window for a long time, gazing at the moon and thinking of her father. Frothy clouds lit by moonlight moved steadily across the sky. The rest of her world was dark because of the cover of the thick aspen wood. She wondered where her father was and if he was still alive. At times, she thought she could hear his voice.

"Ella," he would say in a laugh as he ran to her and swung her up and around in his arms. They used to walk together through the wood. There was a spot near the top of the mountain where an old willow grew. The tree was her father's favorite in the entire wood. He would lift Ella up and place her on a branch. Then he would tell her the legend of the trees.

"This tree," he would say, "is my tree. It has been around since the day I came into the world.

And it will always be here—growing and changing—as long as I am still alive upon the earth."

And then he would become earnest. "The trees, Ella, are so important. They are a part of us. We all have a tree to take care of. You can keep a tree alive by the way that you live. And there is a tree that, as long as it is allowed to grow, will keep you alive."

Ella thought about the old willow and the words of her father until she fell asleep.

2

The next morning, Ella woke early to avoid the cries of Katrina and Beatrice. She changed into her only dress—which now came to several inches above her ankle and was snug in the arms, waist, and chest—wrapped a cream-colored shawl around her shoulders, and crept through the creaking front door. She walked to the top of the mountain to visit the old willow, sat at the trunk, and looked up at the tree. It was still alive, even if it wasn't flourishing as it once had been.

It had been only a year since she'd last seen her father, but the tree had begun to wither long before that. Even while her father lingered, Ella had watched his tree show less life in the spring and shed fewer leaves in the fall. Some of the wilting branches now touched the ground.

But still, it was alive. She hoped that meant her father was still somewhere, still alive, and if somehow the evil was taken from him, he would return as he once was.

Ella blamed the prince for what had happened to her father. Rumors of his evil and deceit could be heard in any shop of the village, and Ella knew he had been in her house that night. But what or who could take that evil away, she did not know, and this helplessness had over the years nearly drowned her hope.

Ella walked for the rest of the day, knowing that Cinder would be gone for most of it. It did not bother her to be alone, since it was a pleasant alternative to being with the people she knew. And briefly, as she thought of her father, a few traitorous tears crept down her cheeks.

But for the most part, the slow, simple walk calmed Ella. The woods were a place she could feel solace and peace no matter what was troubling her. She knew, however, that they were also a place where anyone could cause a stir in secrecy, and often where trouble and evil were birthed. And so she walked with caution.

Ella returned home by the light of the moon and entered her house to find a scene much like the day before.

"There you are, you little good-for-nothing." Katrina was trying on her new shoes. "There. Perfect. Mother, don't they look perfect?"

Mother stopped spinning for a moment to look at the shoes. Ella glared. She was positive that their mother wouldn't stop spinning even if Ella was on fire, but she always had time to look at some silly thing Katrina was doing.

"Yes, darling. You look perfect. You are very beautiful." The mother returned to her spinning as she began to yell. "Cinderella! The child! You must come take the child!"

Cinder came down the stairs. It looked to Ella as though she had a secret. "Did you have a pleasant day?" Cinder asked before fulfilling her mother's request.

"Yes. I walked to the willow," Ella replied.

Cinder was torn from Ella's words by a fit from Beatrice.

"Cinderella! Take your sister away so I can spin! If I do not spin, we will have nothing to eat." Their mother began to cry but continued to spin as Cinder took Beatrice upstairs.

"Did she thank you for the shoes?" Ella watched Cinder tuck Beatrice in bed after singing her a song. It wasn't until Beatrice was asleep that the two sisters could finally spend time together each day.

"Does she ever thank anyone for anything?" Cinder asked back with a smile.

"You take too much, Cinder. You do too much for them."

"I don't mind. I hope father will come back someday, and in the meantime I do my part."

"What's my part, Cinder?"

Cinder looked down at the bed that they both sat on. Beatrice was grinding her teeth between them. Even though the three of them shared the bed, the one Katrina had to herself was just as large.

"Ella, dear sister . . . I walked farther than the village today. I went to the walls outside the kingdom castle." Her voice was excited but leery.

Ella looked at her sister in shock. "How did you ever return before I did? That is a full day's walk!"

"I ran part of the way, and a nice man gave me a ride in his carriage."

"Why did you go to the kingdom castle?"

Cinder continued in a deep whisper. "A woman in the village told me that the king and queen are looking for castle servants. I would have a few responsibilities, but I would also have opportunities . . . to learn."

"But you would have to live at the castle."

"I would have to live there for six days of the week, Ella. Then I could come home to you."

The two stared at each other in silence.

"Ella, I hoped that you would be able to stay and help with Mother and our sisters. This is a great opportunity for me. I will make almost as much as Father did when he was alive."

"Father is still alive!"

"I'm sorry, Ella. I believe he is alive as well. It only slipped out. Please forgive me." Cinder waited patiently for her sister to calm. "Please allow me to do this."

"I would never stop you from anything that would bring you happiness. I will do my best." Ella knew better than to make any promises or to express that she could not make any promises. If Cinder had any intimation that Ella might not take her place, she would never go to the kingdom castle.

Ella's hollow voice and unspoken words echoed inside her own head. She received a hug from a giddy Cinder.

"Oh, Ella, I am happy. The king's high adviser already gave me the position today. I am so happy for your answer. I must leave early in the morning."

A tear escaped from Ella's eye, slipped down her cheek, and fell onto her white nightgown.

"But I have made you unhappy. I can see that. Dear Ella, don't be distraught. Everything will be all right."

"I am not unhappy." Ella wiped the tear away and produced a smile. "I will only miss you. That is all. You do not need to worry about me."

It was a lie, but sisters often tell each other lies in order to protect either themselves or the other. Ella was trying to protect Cinder from worry, since they each had plenty of that already.

But after Cinder extinguished the candle that night, Ella was left to hold the worry in her own heart all alone. She could not imagine that even her best would be enough to satisfy Katrina and Beatrice. And the thought of the atrocities that would soon cumber her (all of which she would have to bear alone) was overwhelming.

Ella listened to the sounds of her sisters sleeping, and while there would be more room in the bed, she wondered how she would ever manage without her Cinder.

As the young woman of only sixteen stared out the small bedroom window into the night sky, no internal commitments were made, no unspoken promises to herself or her mother or sisters were given. She simply thought to herself all the night that she would tolerate it as long as she was able.

3

When Ella woke the next morning from what brief sleep her spinning mind had allowed, Cinder was gone. And Beatrice was already out of bed. Ella walked down the stairs to find her mother working and occasionally placing food into Beatrice's mouth. They looked ridiculous to Ella. Beatrice was not blooming yet, but she was no longer a child, either. Katrina was brushing her hair while she looked in the mirror.

"There there, dear," Adela said to her youngest daughter. "Cinderella will be up soon, and I'm sure she'll take you out in the fresh air for a walk."

Ella walked into the middle of the room, where she was certain they all could see her, but nobody noticed.

"I will take you, Beatrice."

Beatrice looked at Ella and scowled.

"Cinderella!" Mother called. "Your sister needs you."

"And tell her that I must have three of my dresses mended," Katrina added.

"Cinderella!" Ella's mother never stopped working through all of this except to place a piece of bread in Beatrice's mouth.

Ella took a few steps forward. "I am here, Mother. Come, Beatrice. I will take you outside."

Beatrice stuck her tongue out at Ella and then turned to her mother with her mouth open wide to ask for another morsel.

Ella watched them all for a moment. She spoke louder this time. "Mother, Cinder isn't here. But I am . . . Ella."

"Cinderella!" Adela screamed.

Ella didn't understand why her mother would not acknowledge her. She knew that Beatrice could see her, at least, because she kept pulling the oddest and most unattractive faces at her, one of which included a finger or two up her nostrils. But the others ignored her.

"Cinderella!" Mother called one last time.

Ella stood in confusion but she was intelligent enough that she could guess. Her mother had forgotten her. Or, at least, had combined her and Cinder together so that there was only Cinderella—the servant. Ella no longer existed to her mother at all. She wasn't even sure if her mother could hear her. Ella wondered when she had slipped from her mother's memory. It had been a long time since they had spoken to each other or even looked at each other.

"Katrina, what has happened to Mother? Why can't she hear me?" Ella asked.

"Mother, tell Cinderella to come now! My dresses need mending. This one looks awful." Katrina adjusted her bustline and moved her face closer to the mirror to inspect her full lips.

Ella looked at Katrina in the mirror, but Katrina paid no attention. Ella considered for a moment what to do next. She didn't think that her mother could handle the news that Cinder was not coming back for days. She wasn't even sure if the spinning woman would understand or hear her words. Perhaps her mother wouldn't even be able to see the small but sturdy girl if she were standing directly in front of her or if she sat down on top of the pile of yarn that was being spun. She wasn't about to get a rise out of Katrina or a fit out of Beatrice, and since none of them seemed to know that she was there—breathing, talking, waiting—aside from the little brat, Ella turned around and walked out the door with nothing but the clothes covering her.

The third daughter of Weston and Adela of Willow Top walked in the cool morning's mountain breeze. She walked through the rays of the afternoon sun that split among all of the trees. The aspens that were so familiar to her began to thin as she walked into a part of the forest she wasn't sure she had ever been in. A variety of trees grew here, including oaks, birches, blue spruces, and even a few cherry trees that provided her with nourishment. She continued as the light of day dimmed until it turned to blackness. And alone in the forest, Ella sat beside a tree until the next morning.

4

Sometimes, when there is a need, just the right person will come by to fill it, as if destiny were guiding them. That is exactly what happened for Ella. She was in need. And before she even woke, someone who could fill the need came by.

The wheels of an old, dusty carriage spun clumsily. The road was bumpy, making the speed of the carriage even slower as each wheel took its turn dipping deep into the hardened grooves in the soil.

The dark-haired man driving the carriage was middle-aged. The reins were cradled in his hands and then hung loosely by his bent legs. He pulled the horses to a stop and stood.

Ella was still sleeping when the man thudded to the ground from the carriage and carefully approached her.

"Miss? Miss, are you all right?"

Ella's mind began to wake, but her eyes remained glued shut.

"Miss?"

Ella tried to open her eyes as the sound of a strange voice drew closer and closer. She finally peeled them open and, upon seeing the man, pulled her shawl tightly around her until she remembered that she wasn't in night clothes.

The man looked at her with a strange, confused sort of look. "Are you all right, miss? Have you been out here all night?"

"Yes, sir. I got lost in the wood." Ella sat up a little straighter and rubbed at one of her eyes.

"Do you know your way now? Can you find your way back home?" He had to grab on to the reins again because the horses were trying to resume their journey.

"I'm not going back home, sir. I guess in that case, I don't really know which way to go." Ella looked up and down the road. Nothing was familiar to her.

The man continued to look down at her where she sat. He considered in what way he could be of the best service to her.

"My wife and I . . . uh . . . well, my business has become prosperous, and just last night, my wife and I discussed the possibility of being able to afford a servant. We have two little children that my wife could use some help looking after, and there are, of course, the typical household chores. I am on my way back home now, if you would like to come and speak to my wife."

He did not look like one of the men from her village, with their caramel hair and blue eyes. His dark hair—which framed his face like two symmetrical curtains—and dark eyes reminded her of her mother. He was tall and strong. And while his clothing was filthy, there was nothing about him that appeared to be harmful or that caused the hairs on her arm to stand upright. Ella stared back for a time while she thought of what to say. Should she go with the stranger? He seemed sincere.

Ella sat up straight to be direct with her question. "Are your children happy, sir . . . and loved?"

"I beg your pardon, miss. I don't believe I understand your question."

"You and your wife . . . do you love your children? And take care of them the best that you can?"

"Why, of course we do. We have a son and a daughter. They are both a bit rambunctious, but my wife is simply feeling a little run down and could use some extra help. If you would like to decline or if you have somewhere else that you are going . . ."

"I don't need much, sir. Just a little to eat, and perhaps enough to buy myself a new dress someday."

"That should be manageable, miss." The man now held the reins tight to prevent the carriage from moving ahead any farther.

Ella stood. "Could you teach me to read? I would take even less if you could offer me schooling."

The man smiled. "Yes, I could teach you to read, or my wife could. You would be very welcome."

Ella gave the man one last searching look before she put her trust in the stranger. Then after he climbed up onto the carriage, she followed.

5

The man introduced himself as Paul Robinson and explained that he was in the business of building bridges across the river to make transportation and trade in the kingdom more efficient. He had been hired by the king's high advisor three years ago, and there was no end in sight as far as connecting the kingdom was concerned; many parts of the river were too wide for crossing without a bridge. He had spent the night at one of the sites and was on his way home when he found Ella on the side of the road.

They traveled in the carriage for hours, and Ella wondered if the wheels would stay attached or not. She jolted about for the long ride to the man's cottage. Ella listened to him speak for the whole ride.

His smile caused Ella to smile herself, and he even had her laughing a time or two.

As they reached the cottage that was only slightly bigger than her family's home, Ella grew nervous. If for some reason Paul's wife did not accept her, she had traveled all that way for nothing and would have no hope of finding her way back to Willow Top or anywhere else. Paul jumped down from the carriage and tied up the horses. He reached a hand out for Ella to help her down and then led her to the front door. The sun was low enough that shadows now covered the entire ground.

Paul and Ella walked up the three, half-log steps and into his home. "Fern," called Paul. He turned to Ella to wink and whisper, "She'll be pleased to see you."

A woman with red, curvy hair stepped into the living space from the kitchen. She dried her hands on the bulk of the red apron that was tied around her small waist. "And who is this—a mistress?" she teased.

"Of course not, love." Paul kissed his wife on the cheek, holding a handful of her hair and face. "This is Ella. She is looking for work, and since we had discussed finding some help, I thought I would bring her home for you to look over."

"Well, she's just adorable."

Paul smiled at Ella, amused that his wife would care first for how she looked.

"How old are you, Ella?"

"I'll be seventeen in four months." Ella was trying to disguise her shyness. The woman's pleasant look helped her to be bolder than usual. Securing this job suddenly meant everything to her.

The two children burst into the room, laughing and playing with twigs from aspen trees. Ella watched them, leery of a foul look to come from one of their small, pudgy faces or a tantrum to erupt. They both looked at her and smiled. Ella smiled back.

"You look hungry, Ella," the woman said.

"Of course she is hungry," said Paul. "As am I. I was out of food by the time I found her and was too anxious to get home to stop." He kissed his wife again.

"We were holding supper until Paul arrived, and there is plenty. Then I would be grateful if you helped me get the children bathed and ready for bed. If you seem skilled to me by then, I think an arrangement can be made."

"See there, Ella? The woman doesn't waste any time." Ella looked at Paul and smiled. He kissed his wife and children and disappeared to a back room to prepare for supper.

Ella was naturally a hard worker. With Fern praising her about how well she cleaned up after dinner and prepared the bathwater, the work became a joy to her. She got the children bathed and dressed in their bedclothes, after which they all sat on the floor and listened to Fern read the words of a book with color and feeling. To Ella, it was like listening to a song or watching a dance by the light of an outside fire or walking barefoot through a creek.

Ella watched as Fern tucked the children into their beds. Paul came upstairs to shake and rattle the mattresses as the children bounced up and down with giggles and squawks of pleasure.

"Ella," Fern began as the three sat in front of the night fire. Ella loved how she spoke—sweet, direct, as if Ella was her equal. "You did well tonight. We would be pleased if you would stay with us. We do not have an extra bedroom, only a small floor space where we store food. But Paul can make an excellent mattress, and I will make sure he gets it done before he goes off again."

Paul looked at his wife as he rocked in his chair and said, "Yes, love."

A full day's work commenced the following morning. The children were up even before the sun, and there was feeding, mending, washing . . . even Ella's first lessons began that day.

Ella enjoyed the children immensely. Benny was six and had the blondest hair she had ever seen. His eyes were the same color as the sky when the sun first comes up in the morning. Maybelle was exactly a year and seven days younger, and there was something about her chubby, dimpled cheeks and lingering baby face that caused Ella to dote on her immediately, taking extra long to comb her hair and holding her even when she was clearly old enough to walk and run almost as fast as her brother.

Benny and Maybelle did everything together and for the most part were easily managed. Ella played with them in the morning after breakfast and then helped Fern with the chores in the afternoon. Her lessons were in the evening after the children had gone to bed. Fern had her start on a ragged book, and the flickering candle sat so close to it that an occasional drip of wax fell on the page.

Ella and Fern quickly became the best of friends and found much pleasure working together. They often laughed as one swept and the other washed dishes and would tease Paul whenever he walked out the door or came through it. Fern took Ella with her when she went into the town square to purchase goods and introduced her to everyone she knew, especially the young men. It was not long before Ella was sought after by many of the town's young people, and Fern would often give her the afternoon off to enjoy some activity with people her own age.

Paul and Fern took turns in the evenings teaching Ella about all of the subjects they could, and Ella in turn taught the children in the daytime what she had learned, so as to make her understanding concrete by passing it on to someone else.

Ella's favorite subject was geography. The only places she had ever known about were her own family cottage, the village closest to their home, and the kingdom castle. She was learning that each village and surrounding territory had a name. She learned that she had moved further away from the kingdom castle, to a place called Riverwood.

The river was so close that Ella could hear it at all times, even when the children were playing loudly near her. Ella loved the sound of the river, and it soon became the thing she felt closest to. It sang her to sleep at night, walked with her in the forest, listened to her troubled heart, and knew all her secrets.

Riverwood was a small village, and the residents were all kind to Ella even though she was a servant. She soon made several friends; her favorites were two sisters named Amelia and Constance, who looked so much alike with their blonde hair, blue eyes, and flat faces, that Ella had trouble telling them apart at first.

There was even a young man that began to charm Ella a bit. Leander was only having a bit of fun, but it was Ella's first time being friends with a boy, and his company and attentions were exciting to her. He would place wildflowers behind her ear and hold her hand when Amelia and Constance weren't looking.

They would all have picnics at a place where the river formed a great waterfall, and once, when the other girls were looking over the great gush of water, Leander leaned across the picnic blanket and kissed a blushing Ella on the center of her right cheek. But Ella would not be around long enough to really get to know any of them. In fact, the all-too-short summer months were all that Ella would be allowed such leisure.

When her work was done and her friends had all returned home, Ella would often seek solitude by the river to think about her family. She thought of the old willow, of her mother spinning, of her self-absorbed and tormented sisters, and of Cinder, who by now certainly knew of Ella's absence and had perhaps even accepted it.

6

Cinder fidgeted for the entire ride home after her first week of kingdom castle duty. Life at the castle had been much more demanding than she had ever anticipated. She had to wake very early, complete her studies, work in each department for an hour—laundry, gardens, cleaning, latrines, cooking, and personal aides—take care of her own laundry and other needs, review her studies, and try to sleep, despite how worried she was about Ella and the rest of her family.

Castle servants were required to find their own way home, but luckily for Cinder, she had met a fellow servant who lived in the closest village. It was a bit out of her way, but the girl insisted on helping her get home for her day off. When the coach neared the cottage, a horrible cry arose from inside the house. Cinder jumped out even as the coach was still in motion, thanked her new friend, and ran up the walk and through the door. Panting for breath, she entered to find a disturbing scene.

Katrina was pulling Beatrice's hair while Beatrice was kicking and hitting. They were both screaming at each other. Their mother was spinning as tears dripped and dropped onto her lap and splashed onto the spinning wheel, wetting the freshly made yarn.

Katrina had redecorated. Every piece of furniture was in a different spot—the redwood lounge sat where their father's desk used to be, and the desk was under the window facing the outside of the house. She had even hung up a few self-portraits. Only the mother and her spinning wheel remained untouched.

While Katrina's changes were fairly tasteful, Beatrice had left an unwelcome mark. The cottage was a mess of large and small food crumbs, dirty and clean clothes, and significant and insignificant family belongings, ranging from kitchen utensils to jewelry that had been passed down from their grandmothers.

Cinder rushed to her mother's side. "Mother!" she exclaimed. "What has happened?"

"Cinderella, why did you not come down? I have been calling for you all of these days. Why have you not come down?"

Cinder looked at the side of her mother's face. Her mother continued to cry and spin.

"Mother! What happened to Ella? Where is Ella?"

The mother finally looked at her daughter. "What are you talking about? Why did you not come? Your sisters have needed you."

Cinder ran up the stairs as her sisters continued their quarrels. When she opened the door to the room she and Ella had shared for so long, she saw a scene similar to the one downstairs. The window had been broken, the curtains were torn, and the thin covers on the bed were in disarray. Cinder listened as the cries from below continued to find their way to her ears. She called out the window for her sister. When that produced no answer, she ran down the stairs amid cries of "Cinderella! Cinderella!" and "Mother, she's biting me on the arm!"

Cinder left the cottage, but the closed door did not shut out the commotion. The summer air was warm, and the aspen trees shook their leaves in the slight wind.

"Ella!" she called again and again. She walked around the house and up the mountain a ways, but with no success of finding her sister.

As Cinder walked up the steps of the cottage once more, the sounds of the struggle indoors began to diminish. She opened the door with a great feeling of despair. Beatrice had fallen asleep with Katrina's hair still in her firm grasp. Cinder helped Beatrice up the stairs to bed, after which Katrina was calmed and groomed. The mother spun and spun, looking wearier than ever. Once everything was calm and the house had been put back in relative order, Cinder waited outside until dark for her sister to come home. But when Cinder left early the following morning for the kingdom castle, there had been no sign of Ella.

The coach driver loaded Cinder's slight bag and held a hand out to help her aboard. Cinder's gray hair waved as she held her head out of the coach to look for her sister. Ella was nowhere to be found.

7

Life at the kingdom castle became much more difficult as burdensome thoughts of what might have happened to Ella weighed heavily on Cinder's mind. In order to escape these thoughts, or at least to hold them off as she completed her tasks each day, Cinder became the best worker in the castle. Every movement of her hands and feet was intensified, making her faster, more efficient, and much noted among her equals as well as her superiors. But when she tried to sleep at night, her dreams were dark and haunted by memories both good and bad, as well as imaginations of Ella's death or entrapment.

There was a knight named Tanner whose duty it was to guard the halls in the castle at night with his fellows. This particular knight was more observant than the others, and whenever he passed Cinder's room, he heard the cries of an anguished soul. Each time he heard the girl, he felt pity for her. His guard post changed week by week, but every time he was outside Cinder's room, he heard more of the same.

One night, when it was time to walk through the halls of the servants' quarters, Tanner resolved to stop at her door and listen. He was one of two knights stationed in the servant halls that night, and when the other's footsteps were distant, Tanner paused in front of Cinder's door, stretched his neck, and placed his ear against the splintered wood.

"I'm so sorry, Ella. I never should have left you alone. My poor sister is lost, maybe dead. What am I to do without my sister?"

The words troubled the knight. For weeks he pondered them and listened outside Cinder's door whenever he could understand words among the cries. At last, the troubled sobs became more than he could bear, and at sunrise one day, he waited for the girl who made the noise to come out of her room. He was surprised at the silver hair that came with her young face.

"Excuse me, miss . . ." But what was he to say? "My name is Sir Tanner." He stared at her for a few moments before speaking again. "At night, when you sleep . . . you . . ."

Cinder did not want to be rude, but she was late for her morning classes. "I must go, sir. And I'm not entirely sure that you are supposed to speak to me. I am a servant." Cinder turned to leave and walked until he called after her again.

"I hear your cries at night, miss. And I was only wondering if I could be of any service to you . . . and your sister."

The swaying of her light brown servant dress stopped, and the long, ashy hair that Tanner had been watching walk away turned to reveal a solemn face. "I am sorry, sir, that I have disturbed you. But I am afraid that there is nothing that anyone can do now. Thank you for your kind inquiry."

"Where is your sister?"

"I don't know," Cinder replied, her voice sunken and shameful.

"Who is your sister?" Tanner tried to close the distance between them.

"Her name is Ella." Emotion was rising in Cinder's voice, and she began to choke on her words.

"What happened to her?"

"That also I do not know. I came home after my first week at the kingdom castle, and she was gone."

"What does she look like?"

"I am late, sir, and must go. But this much I can tell you, she is very beautiful—with golden hair and golden eyes—and she may be in great trouble, maybe even dead. Good-bye, sir. I will try to sleep better at night."

The knight watched the girl run from his sight. What Cinder had told him concerned him even more than her sorrowful nighttime cries. He knew his duty as a knight and immediately sought counsel from one of the king's low advisors.

Tanner left the servants' quarters and walked to the other side of the castle. Lord Tracey was the first low advisor he came across, seated at a rectangular table inside a meeting room. He was poring over parchments that were trying to roll back up again.

Tanner cleared his throat. "Excuse me, Lord Tracey."

The man looked up to acknowledge Tanner, then as he turned back to his work asked, "What is it, Tanner?" Lord Tracey's long, curly hair fell to cover his face. His hands were large and rough-looking, and he wore a long, olive robe.

Tanner took a few steps closer to him. "There is a maiden, your grace—a very fair maiden—who is lost in the kingdom. Is it not my duty, now that I know of the girl, to try to help her? She may be in grave danger."

"What is the girl's name?" asked Lord Tracey as he continued to study the writings before him.

"Her name is Ella, and she is the sister of the servant Cinder, who works here in the kingdom castle."

Lord Tracey turned to look at Tanner once more. All of the aides and advisors knew of Cinder's work at the kingdom castle. "I will speak to my brother advisors, and we will make a decision soon."

"Please, your grace. Do hurry."

The king's low advisor could see the anxiety in the knight's eyes, and being a good man, he agreed to do his best in the matter. He waved an arm to dismiss Tanner, and Tanner left the room.

8

Tanner had to listen to Cinder's muffled cries one more time, as it wasn't until his next turn guarding the servant halls that Lord Tracey came to him with an answer. Had it taken any longer, Tanner would have sought him out, but in the middle of that first night back in the hallways of the servants' quarters, Lord Tracey came with two other men.

"Your request is granted, sir. It took longer than expected; the prince is always very thorough before he will lend one of his knights for a quest."

"The prince? You took this matter to the prince?"

"Yes, sir. That was the advice from my brother advisors."

Sir Tanner looked at Lord Tracey with suspicious eyes. Prince Monticello was full of darkness and black magic. "You could have granted permission yourself. Why did you take this matter to the prince?"

"The prince oversees everything that we do as low advisors. It is his job. Prince Monticello receives all of the questions and affairs that are brought to us. We are required to keep no secrets from him."

"This is a simple matter with one of the subjects in his kingdom. Has the law changed? You used to have the power to make many decisions on your own, or at least in your councils."

"No matter, Tanner. I have given you the only answers that I have to give." He held out a rolled parchment. "Here are your papers. Two of the prince's personal aides will be accompanying you. They are well-educated and skilled with the sword."

The hesitant knight took the scroll bearing the prince's seal from the lord.

"This is Flesher," Lord Tracey said as he pointed to the man on his right. Sir Tanner looked into the man's serious eyes, but the man only stared into the long hallway. Flesher was tall with broad shoulders and a large, pointed nose.

"And this is William." The knight looked at the mischievous face of the shorter and fatter of the two men. He had curly hair and small blue eyes.

"Oh, and by the way, I did some research on the girl and nothing is known of her whereabouts or of her family except that her sister works here in the castle."

Sir Tanner placed his hand over his heart to signal to Lord Tracey that he was leaving, but Tracey leaned in and whispered, "Your time is short. You only have until the next full moon. If you do not find her by then, your quest will be over and the prince will pronounce her dead. But if you are successful, you will be rewarded beyond measure." Their eyes met, and Sir Tanner became even more apprehensive.

Tanner led Flesher and William down the hallway and outside. The aides gathered supplies while Tanner readied the horses. Once they rode through the gate of the kingdom castle, their quest had begun.

Cinder was brought before the prince on the very same day. Her head nearly touched the ground when she bowed to him.

"Please, stand," Prince Monticello said in a chillingly quiet voice that she quickly obeyed.

"What can I do for your majesty?"

The prince stood from his pine writing desk and walked closer to the shaking girl.

"I have heard good reports of you, Cinder of Willow Top. Tell me, do you know of a man, also from Willow Top, named Weston?"

Cinder looked at her inquirer with curious eyes. "Yes, your majesty. My father's name is Weston."

"Is it? He is at your home, I presume?" The prince's voice was full of deceit, but the trusting girl did not notice.

"No, your majesty. We do not know where he is, or if he is even alive." Cinder's head drooped toward the stone floor. The prince's chamber was dark, with only one small window, but she could still see the grooves of each cut of stone.

"That is dreadful news. And your sister? She is also lost?" He put a finger to his thoughtful face and tilted his head to one side as he waited for her response.

The lowly subject turned red where she stood and her skin became hot. "How do you know that?"

"My dear, it is my business to know of every affair in the kingdom. A quest has been sent forth to ensure her safe return."

Cinder looked at the prince admiringly. "Can it really be?" She stared at him, her mouth and eyes open in disbelief.

"Perhaps we may be able to do something about your father as well."

"My father? It all seems impossible, good prince. Is it really so?"

The prince walked closer to Cinder and reached a hand out to stroke her face. "Nothing is impossible. And I always speak only the truth. I will see to it personally."

The young girl felt all at once glad for his soft touch, uncomfortable at his closeness, and overwhelmed with joy at his words. Her eyes became damp. The prince took a step back and spoke again, this time with a voice more for business.

"I have heard of your good work here at the kingdom castle. I would like to make you mistress of managing affairs. You will be responsible for the coordination of all the servants as well as the personal aides."

"Your majesty . . ." she spoke up quickly, "truly I am grateful—overcome, even—by your words, but I do not feel adequate—"

"Shhhh," he said as he put a finger to her lips and resumed his calm, luring tone. "I am sure you will exceed all my expectations. Go now. Finish your work as scheduled today, and tomorrow you will begin your new tasks. I will send for you when I have word of your sister."

Cinder fell to her knees and kissed the prince's hand. Then her silver hair flew behind her as she ran from the chamber.

9

Sir Tanner and the prince's aides sat around a great fire. The glowing orange flame was the only thing in the company that held any warmth.

"Stop making that horrible racket," Tanner said to William.

William's evil smile was enough to make all the hairs on Tanner's body stand on end. He was scraping the bones of his fish along any surface that made an interesting sound. First it was his sword, followed by a rock and stick, and finally his own armor. Tanner glared at him with a hardened face.

"How long are we going to drag out this pointless quest to find this pointless girl? Time is precious to a man who has many women to spoil and much wine to drink." William's head moved with a drunken sway.

"No quest is pointless. It has been obvious from the moment we met that the prince's aides either have no code of conduct or have made no oath to keep it, but you make that clearer with each movement of your drunken limbs and ugly tongue."

William's small eyes turned black behind the fire's glow. His smile faded, and he spoke in a soft, gruff voice. "Oh, we have our codes and oaths. I imagine they're just different from yours."

"How much longer, really?" Flesher asked, glaring at William. He wrapped his arms tightly around himself and shivered. "We've been gone for three weeks already."

The moon shone brightly overhead, even to men blinded by fire.

"Riverwood is our last stop," Tanner answered. "We will be there by tomorrow at the end of the day."

William abruptly shot out his last few swallows of wine. "'Bout sent that bit to my lungs," he said as the other men wiped their faces. "I don't think they would appreciate a drink as well as my belly does, even if it is wine as fine as this." William held up his bottle and laughed. He tried to stand but fell back down. His curls bounced up and down at the sides of his head.

"I'll take guard for him tonight," Flesher offered to Tanner. The two men had both taken on extra responsibilities over the weeks and were both tired of William's absent presence.

"Thank you. I'm going to try to get some sleep." Tanner wrapped a wool blanket around his shoulders and lay close to his horse on a bed of twigs and leaves.

But Sir Tanner hadn't slept well for the last two and a half weeks. Just a few short days into their journey, another knight had brought word from the prince. It was sealed and confidential—only for the eyes of his personal aides. There was no hope of trusting them after that. He slept lightly, watched closely, and listened carefully.

The sun was beginning to cower behind the distant hills, giving way to the darkness of the nighttime sky. Ella sat, lingering on the riverbank. She tossed a pebble into the water and watched as the ripples spread out and almost reached her feet that were dangling over the edge of the bank. A light breeze came from the trees behind her and ruffled her lilac dress. The thought of the warmth in her new home called her back to the wood.

Her feet stepped deliberately on the path back to the Robinson's cottage. There was no more work to be done. The children would be in bed soon after dinner, and Ella was looking forward to a pleasant evening beside the fire with her dearest friends.

Ella smiled as she passed several local villagers.

"Good evening, Miss Ella," said one as they passed each other along the road home.

"Good evening, Frederick. Will your children be playing in the meadow tomorrow?"

"I believe so," the man said as he continued on.

"Tell your wife I will bring Benny and Maybelle so they will have playmates," she called over her shoulder.

The small cottage came into view as Ella approached. Steaming carrots and onions sent their aroma out the windows to greet her. Several horses tied up at the trees outside the home caught her attention as well.

Footsteps and giggles sounded from the trees to the side of the cottage as a pebble landed in front of Ella's feet. Ella looked to see where the noise had come from when Amelia, Constance, and Leander came out of the trees. The girls burst into laughter, and Leander winked at her.

"We got you!" Constance squealed. She looked to Amelia and Leander. "She already looks kind of pale. Maybe she won't last the night." Her laugh was infectious, and Ella couldn't help but break into a hearty one herself.

"Shhhhhh," Amelia cautioned, her face growing darker as the sun sank deeper and deeper into the earth. "You'll scare the ghosts away."

"What are you three up to?" Ella asked, her eyes now showing a lack of trust.

"Just a little fun." Leander gave her another wink. "In the graveyard. Want to come?"

"I don't know if Paul and Fern would allow it." Ella glanced at the horses, curious as to where they had come from.

Leander took a few steps closer to her. "They're from the kingdom castle," he said, pointing to the image on the saddles.

"How do you know that?" Constance asked.

"Look there," he said, still pointing. "It's the crest of the king." The crest had two swords crossed behind a large, white, fig tree.

"They must be here to take you to the castle, Ella. Maybe for the prince's next ball," Constance teased.

Ella looked at Leander and spoke softly. "Why do you think they are here?"

"I don't know. I only know the crest because I saw it when I went with my father to the kingdom castle several years ago. I remember one of the stable hands telling me about the crest and the significance of the tree. Do you know the legend of the trees?" He was feeling quite smart and was eager to impress her.

"Yes. My father told me from the time I was a small child."

Disappointed at her answer, Leander decided to change the subject. "We'll wait for you to ask Paul and Fern if you can come with us."

A large smile covered Ella's face as she walked through the door. "I'm home," she called, expecting a rush of tiny footsteps to approach her.

"Ella, dear, these men have come from the kingdom castle," Fern said as she rose from a wooden chair, her slight wrinkles settling into the places they took when she was concerned or anxious. She wasn't wearing her apron like she usually was when Ella came home in the evenings.

Too many pairs of eyes were focused solely on Ella, and she grew uneasy. The men were all large to her and their faces unfamiliar and dark in the growing night. They were armed with swords, and one of them wore a tunic with the same crest she had seen on the saddle outside. The other two wore black and a deep purple, and the one with curly hair caused an inexplicable fear to rise inside her.

"They have news of your sister," Paul piped up. "They have come to take you to the castle."

"What has happened to my sister?" Ella's eyes flashed over each of the men.

"Nothing, miss," Tanner assured her. "Your sister is concerned about you. We have come to find you and return you to your home."

"This is my home now. You may tell my sister that I am well. You may even tell her where I am, but I will not be coming with you."

Flesher stood up, holding the secret scroll in his hand toward her.

"We have orders from the prince, miss . . . to bring you back to the kingdom castle, even if we have to arrest you."

Ella looked at the rolled parchment that the stranger held in his hand. It was sealed with a menacing black letter M. "But why? What have I done?" she protested.

"It doesn't matter what you have done, miss." William was poking his teeth with a small, pointy stick. "What matters is that the prince has given orders involving us . . . and involving you."

"Don't you want to return to your sister?" Tanner asked, although he was surprised at the news of having to return her to the prince.

Shame appeared in Ella's saddened eyes and frowning face, but no answer escaped her lips; she loved Cinder but did not want to return. A single tear escaped from the corner of her eye.

Paul rose to his feet, and both he and Fern brought their arms around Ella to encircle her completely.

"Don't worry, dear." Fern stroked Ella's long, stringy, windblown hair. "You must go with them, but we want you back as soon as you are permitted." Fern retrieved a package from the table. "I've packed a few of your things."

Ella's eyes began to overflow. She knew that everything she owned would have fit in the package. She glanced at the children, who were playing quietly on the floor. They looked confused and troubled. Not being able to bear the good-bye any longer, Ella turned and walked out the door.

Her three friends had been listening. Their solemn, worried faces did not comfort Ella.

"Ella, where are you going?" Leander asked. Amelia and Constance had grown shy in the presence of the castle men.

The lump in Ella's throat would not allow her to respond.

"Where are you taking her?" Leander was determined to get an answer from someone.

"Don't worry, boy. We'll take good care of her." Nobody liked the way William said it.

Tanner came from behind to whisper to Ella. "You should say good-bye. We need to get moving."

Ella embraced Amelia and Constance, who, aside from a few words of parting, remained speechless. Neither Ella nor Leander quite knew how to say good-bye to each other. The little extra attention he had given her had been in secret.

"Good-bye, Ella," was the only thing he could come up with.

"Good-bye," she said to them all. Ella locked eyes with Leander for a moment before walking to the horses.

Each of Ella's friends waved and said good-bye one last time, Leander lingering for a moment before turning and chasing after the others.

"Thought the good-byes would never end," William said, which produced glares from his two other companions as well as from Ella.

The knight and the prince's two aides joined her in front of the horses.

Ella's hand slid down the nose of a light brown mare.

Tanner introduced himself as well as the other two men. Ella would not look at him.

"Her name is Cassandra," Tanner said, indicating the horse. He wanted to get as much of a glimpse of Ella's face as the darkness would allow. He had traveled a long way to find the girl with golden hair and eyes.

"I don't understand why you are taking me away." Ella's voice was soft, but all the men could hear that she had begun to cry.

"Oh, stop! We don't have to listen to this all the way, do we?" blurted William.

Tanner slipped the package from her hands and placed it inside one of the bags hanging from the horse. "I'll help you up, miss," Tanner said, holding out a hand for her.

Ella awkwardly mounted the horse, and Tanner got on behind her. She didn't like any of it. Her lavender dress that Fern had picked out came up to her knees as she straddled the horse. This bothered her even in the dark. Feeling the presence of a strange man behind her made her nervous. He smelled of earth and fire, much like Paul smelled when he came home after days of working without having had a bath.

Not wanting to lean on the knight and not wanting his arms around her, Ella leaned forward and held onto the horse's mane. She was most uncomfortable and felt as though she would fall off.

"Are you all right, miss?" Tanner whispered.

"I'm sorry. I haven't been on a horse since I was a small child." Her voice was shaky.

"You haven't? Really?"

"No, sir."

"Well, then I'll let you ride on the horse while I walk at her side. That way, you will be able to become better acquainted with riding. We don't need to travel far tonight—just enough to camp."

William began muttering his disapproval, but Flesher seemed indifferent to the whole situation.

Ella was glad to be alone on the horse but did not become more accustomed to riding. Cassandra seemed annoyed with the way her mane was constantly being tugged at.

"Try to relax, miss. Cassandra is perfectly safe. She will not let you fall, nor will I."

"Please do not speak to me, sir. Let me bear it in silence." Ella was still crying.

"Will you ever stop wailing, woman? It's time you got over it!" William looked to Flesher. "Is she going to cry the entire way back to the castle?"

Flesher gave William a disapproving look.

Ella laid her head down on the horse and silently washed the beast's mane with her tears. Why was she going to the prince? Would she ever see Riverwood again? Would she have to return to her mother and sisters? It was all too much to take in, and while she managed to stifle the noise of crying, she could not stop the tears from coming.

The waxing moon was high in the sky when they arrived at a small clearing. Summer had been like a shy child that year, and the air had grown increasingly cold as they traveled. Flesher began making a fire as soon as he tied up his horse.

"Damn! I'm out of wine. How will I ever make it through the night?" The entire group was growing weary of William's constant complaints.

Tanner helped Ella off the horse but let go of her weak body too soon, and she fell to the ground. She moaned a little as he apologized and helped her to her feet. After preparing a place on the ground for her, Tanner handed her a wool blanket. Once the fire was roaring, Flesher tied some rope and hung a thin cloth to divide the men from the maiden.

"We only have a few more fish. We'll have to get some more food tomorrow," Flesher said as he pulled a basket off of his horse.

"You go hunting for food, and I'll go hunting for wine," William scoffed.

Ella held the blanket close and sat down on the ground.

"It won't be long until the fish are cooked, miss. You must be hungry," Tanner said.

"I don't feel like eating." Ella turned onto her hands and knees, crawled to the other side of the divider, and lay down and closed her eyes. She tried to be quiet, but she couldn't help some sniffing.

"Are you still going on, woman?" William looked at the other men. "Can you believe this?"

Flesher and Tanner ignored him.

Tanner checked on Ella before they ate, but she was silent and he did not want to disturb her. The three men ate their fish as the fire dwindled. There was little conversation, although William occasionally sprang into laughter, song, or idiocy.

"You get guard tonight," Tanner said to William.

"What, did you have to take it last night while I was sleeping among the clouds?"

"We've both taken several nights for you." Flesher's anger was finally beginning to show. "It's your turn." They had begun the journey as comrades, but they were now more like unfriendly acquaintances.

"Oh all right, you cowards. Heaven help us if anything happened on a night when I wasn't on guard anyway, with you two criers." He mumbled some more and then rested his head on a log, his legs stretched out toward the fire.

Tanner pulled a small blanket from his horse, having given Ella his larger one. He took off his boots and unfastened the belt that held his sword. A pile of crumbling leaves became his bed. The blanket rested over the center of his body, and his sword was tightly clenched in his hand.

Ella's breathing was loud and deep now, and the knight rested close to the divider—between her and the other two. He tried to sleep lightly, enough to be somewhat refreshed in the morning but not so deep that he couldn't hear Flesher and William if they spoke or created mischief. William was a poor guard at best, anyway, and Tanner felt much safer awake. When their voices began, Tanner woke easily and heard them conversing.

"Are you awake?" Flesher asked William.

"Course I'm awake, you imbecile. I'm on guard."

"What do you think the prince wants with the girl?"

"I . . . don't . . . care," William said in a ridiculous voice. "The prince sees so many people—too many. Some he has killed, some he has thrown in prison, some he hires, and some he merely talks to.

The girl is right to be scared. Although, I do wish she'd stop crying. My ears will start bleeding as soon as I have to hear her voice again."

"What do you think of Tanner?"

William began poking at the mostly consumed fire while Flesher lay shivering under his blanket. "Dull as an empty bottle, that one. Won't even take a sip. I wouldn't care to fight him, though—serious as he is about his bravery and codes. He might actually be a challenge. I just hope that if I do have to fight him, I'm sober."

"You're never sober," Flesher said, his eyes disapproving.

"Oh, right." After a short silence, William said, "Let's just get back as soon as we can. I could really use a drink."

Flesher glared at him but eventually relaxed and went to sleep.

The dialogue disturbed Tanner. His only desire had been to find Ella and return her to her home and family. He was greatly concerned for her now, knowing that the prince wanted her brought to him, even by force if necessary.

10

Ella shivered the entire night and slept little. When the sky began to lighten, her eyes peeled open and looked out into the shadowy trees. She stayed on her bed, listening to the sounds from the other side of the divider.

The sun invited Tanner to rise with it, and a fire was soon blazing. The words he had heard the night before kept his mind in a constant spin. As a knight, Tanner had taken an oath to help any of the king's subjects who were in need. He did not want to take Ella to the prince, but he knew it would be difficult to escape from the other two, and he had very much set his heart on the prize he had been told he would receive for bringing her back. Considering all of this, he was lost for a solution.

His stares straight into the fire caused him to miss the cold maiden who came to sit across from him.

Ella thought he was staring at her and moved to the side a little. When his gaze did not move with her, she sat more at ease. She watched him for a time. Now that the sun was beginning to light everything, she could see every detail of his appearance. His hair was a few shades darker than her own but a few shades lighter than Paul's or her mother's. It hung loosely from his head, coming down past his eyebrows, but parted slightly to show some of his forehead. While he was certainly older than Leander, he was young enough to make Ella think that he probably hadn't been a knight for long. He still wore the tunic with the white tree on the front.

Flesher began to stir, and he kicked William. "Wake up. You're supposed to be on guard."

William groaned, spoke a slew of words that were impossible to understand, and went back to sleep.

Flesher sat close to Ella as he warmed his hands and feet.

Ella leaned away from him, wishing they would all disappear.

"Are you hungry, miss? There are a few berries in my basket if you would like them."

"No, thank you." Ella did not look at him, still angry over the whole affair. She was traveling with three strange men in a territory that was becoming more and more unfamiliar with every step. She did not even know which direction Riverwood was in anymore. Her eyes began to fill with tears again, but she forced them back.

Tanner finally noticed that Ella was awake and that Flesher was sitting close to her. He jumped to his feet and pulled out his sword. Ella's and Flesher's eyes looked back at him in wonder.

"I thought I heard something." Embarrassed, Tanner turned, put his sword away, and left them by the fire to go find more food.

William woke up while Tanner was gone. Ella felt even more out of place, as it was Tanner who made her feel the least worried. Flesher wasn't much older than Tanner, but his large build was intimidating, and William was despicable. Ella hated everything about him, including his curly hair and especially his gruffness and the malicious look in his eye.

William noticed her red eyes before he even sat across from her and Flesher. "Are you at it already? This is going to be a long day."

Ella, who had not let out a single tear that morning, was quick to respond. She stood up and yelled, "Shut up, you fool! I will not listen to your snide remarks any longer. I will stop crying as soon as you can learn to keep your mouth shut for more than a few seconds at a time."

Flesher stared in shock for a moment and then began laughing.

"It's nice to see your mouth is good for more than just crying." William inspected her closer. "You are also beautiful. I didn't notice last night in the dim light of your little cottage. Your hair falls to your waist, which is most becoming on a young lady. And that dress is lovely. I particularly like the lace at the top."

Ella sat back down and moved closer to Flesher as she looked fiercely at William.

Tanner's footsteps became audible. A large, gray rabbit dangled in his hand as he approached them.

"Good man!" William proclaimed. He began placing more wood on the fire.

The three men ate, but Ella would not even have a sip of water.

"You should take some nourishment," Tanner said to her as he folded up the blanket she had slept with. Everything else had already been strapped to the horses again in preparation to leave.

Ella did not speak. She petted Cassandra as she waited to be lifted onto the horse.

"I'll have to ride with you today." Tanner watched her look into the eyes of his favorite horse.

"I know." Ella was beginning to accept that she had to go back with them. "How shall I ride her, sir?"

"You may decide. I will hold you on no matter how you are seated."

Tanner held out his hand. Ella took it and placed her foot into the stirrup. She was thrown through the air as he lifted with too much force. If her foot had not been firmly caught in the stirrup, she would have fallen off the other side of the horse. The humiliated knight grabbed onto her legs and pulled until she was sitting upright, uttering apologies all the while.

Ella sent an annoyed glare in Tanner's direction. "I hope the prince doesn't want me alive. It would seem that you are out to cause my death."

"I'm sorry," said the tormented knight as William and Flesher laughed in the background.

Ella sat facing to the side. Tanner's arms gripped the reins in front of her, and she jerked in every direction as he pulled himself up on the horse. Some of her shifting was in reaction to his movements, but some came in an attempt to steer clear of his obvious clumsiness.

"You may hold onto me if you'd like. You'll feel more stable."

"Either that or you'll push me off." Ella said it under her breath, but Tanner smiled a little and kicked Cassandra so hard that she jolted to a run. Ella had no choice but to grasp his arm to prevent a fall.

"I need my arm, miss!" Tanner yelled over the pounding hooves of the three horses.

"What?"

"Let go of my arm!"

Ella moved her hands along his arm to his chest. She held tightly to his shirt in an awkward manner until she had to wrap her arms around his body entirely.

Regret for her choice to sit sideways was the only thing she felt until they stopped for a short break at midday. Her legs barely permitted her to move once she was on the ground.

The break was short, and Ella's back side ached so much that when it was time to get back on Cassandra, she felt as though she was sitting on a pile of coal instead of on top of a horse's saddle. Ella had refused to eat once again and was unable to sit up very well, so she faced the front of the horse this time and leaned forward, holding onto Cassandra's mane.

The two of them fit better with her sitting forward. Tanner's arms were held out to either side of her, and she felt them occasionally pressing slightly on the sides of her waist. They rode again for a long time, until the sun at last began to get low.

By the time the company finally stopped, Ella was very weak. She let go of Cassandra's thick, wind-ratted mane but could not open her fists because she had held on so tightly for so long. Tanner easily removed himself from the horse and reached up for Ella. She allowed him to lift her off. The ground was solid beneath her feet, but she felt as if either she or the ground were still moving. Her eyes closed for a moment, and she felt Tanner's hands release her waist. When she had to hold herself up, her head felt fuzzy and the earth moved more and more until she could no longer stand. She swayed to one side and then the other. Tanner was still close by, but by the time he reached his arms out to catch her, she was on her way to the ground.

Rather than break her fall, his flustered attempt to catch her simply provided her with an extra smack on her way down. The knight quickly knelt beside her and tried to lift her head. His hands only succeeded at becoming tangled in her hair. "Flesher, fetch some water!"

Ella remained asleep for some time as Flesher and Tanner tried to get her to take a drink. When she woke, she couldn't remember falling but seemed to become aware that something had happened as she discovered the two men fretting over her.

"Let go of me," she said as she pushed Tanner away. "Let me be. Let me rest."

Ella curled up on the ground next to the horse. Tanner retrieved her blanket and made a bed for the maiden. He prodded her to lie on it. Then he moved Cassandra so she would not step on the maiden.

"You really should eat something, miss. Tell me what you would eat," Tanner whispered as he knelt by her side again.

Ella looked up at him with sleepy eyes and said, "I'm fond of deer meat."

She closed her eyes immediately after, and Tanner allowed a smile to form on half of his lips.

"And deer you shall have," he whispered as he swept a piece of her hair off her face.

Tanner readied his bow and arrow and then began a trek deep into the forest.

"I'll go and get some firewood," Flesher said angrily to William, who was already resting against a tree.

"I'll just sit here and . . . sit."

Flesher gave William a disapproving look before turning to leave. William watched him walk away. When he was out of sight, William turned his eyes to the sleeping girl.

Ella felt darkness begin to cover her as his footsteps approached. She was caught in the reality of being unable to wake from a dream. A hand was placed on her shoulder and caressed it for a moment. Ella struggled inside her mind, forcing herself to wake, until she was staring wide-eyed at William.

"Get your hand off of me." There was no mistaking the forcefulness of her words, but being a fool, William did not react.

"It's all in good fun, miss."

Ella quickly rose to her feet and backed away from him. He followed her playfully. She looked around for the others.

"They're gone. It's just you and me." His slow, mocking voice triggered several emotions in Ella, none of them fear. She changed her direction and stomped toward him. He smiled at her. Ella's feet stopped a little in front of him. She stood calmly for a moment and then kicked him in a most unpleasant way. William gasped and hunched over, holding the place where she had kicked.

Ella had nowhere to run but searched the trees desperately for one of the others.

"Come here, you little whelp," William said once he had recovered. Ella screamed as William grabbed her by the hair and started kissing her face.

Tanner heard the cry and immediately dropped the deer he was carrying on his back. He ran full speed toward the camp.

Flesher also heard the cry. Being closer to the camp, it wasn't long before his sword was pressing into William's back. Ella's head was still being pulled backward.

"You had better stop before the knight gets back." Flesher had produced his darkest and most threatening voice yet.

William put his hands up and turned to face Flesher with a smile. Tanner came upon the sight and wondered what had happened. He saw a frightened Ella, a determined Flesher, and an obnoxious William. Cassandra whinnied as Tanner slowly approached the others.

"What has happened here?"

"We were just sporting a little," William answered, his eyes fixed on Flesher's.

Flesher glared at William for a few more moments and then put his sword away.

William immediately turned to Tanner. "Didn't you get anything? We're starving!"

Tanner was still cautious. "It's back a ways." He had to pause to catch his breath. "Maybe a quarter mile. Go and get it while Flesher and I start the fire."

"I have to do all the work around here," William said as he headed to the wood, smirking once more in Ella's direction.

Tanner looked toward Ella, but she would not look at him.

The fire was soon blazing, just in time for the arrival of night. Ella's mouth watered at the smell of her favorite meat. Water had been her only relief for the last little while, and though she no longer felt thirsty, eating would be the only cure for the faintness she was feeling. Tanner held out some meat in front of her. It was still difficult to take it from him, but her body demanded it. She took tiny bites and, when it was gone, quietly asked for more.

Tanner watched her eat. He sat fairly close to her but moved closer to whisper something. "I'm glad to see you eating."

Ella stopped chewing momentarily but resumed again.

Tanner continued to whisper as he leaned in toward her face. "I will not leave you again. If I have to hunt, you may come with me."

Ella looked directly into his eyes for the first time. They were the same medium brown as his hair, and she saw that a beard was beginning to form on his face. Of all the men she had ever encountered, Ella thought he was the most handsome. "Thank you," she said, and then she shot an accusing glance at William. He was too busy eating to notice.

It was only a day and a half until they would arrive at the castle. The moon was ever growing but not quite full yet. William disappeared for a time the next night, and what was infinitely worse, he returned . . . with wine.

"Where have you been?" Flesher asked when he came back.

William ignored him and pulled three bottles of wine out of his pack.

"No need to thank me. One does what one can."

"Thank you for what?" Tanner's irritation was reaching its peak. "Nobody here is going to thank you for being drunk."

Tanner divided the meat he had been cooking into three, taking the smallest portion for himself and giving Ella and Flesher their share. He knew William didn't eat when there was wine in view.

William drank each bottle dry in no time at all, which was the start of trouble. He moved closer to Ella, who had been trying to avoid any association with him all night.

"Pretty little thing. What do you wager the prince wants with her, Flesher? Your sister is a fine worker. Maybe he wishes to enslave you as well."

Ella did not like him talking about Cinder. Anger was welling up inside her like water in a pot, steaming and shaking just before it boils.

"Of course, I know what I would do with you. I would keep you forever in a cell, where I could have you all to myself."

Tanner stepped closer. "Time for bed, William. Back away from Ella."

"I'm obviously not tired. And look at her. She's full of life." William's speech was slurred, and his hands and arms flew wildly about.

"I saw the face of the last person who was brought before the prince. She was a lot like you—young, very fair. She looked a lot better while she was alive. The prince had her killed."

"That is enough, William! Stop it now!" Flesher was getting involved as well.

Ella looked at Tanner with pleading eyes. "Is that why the prince wants me? To kill me or lock me in prison?"

"I don't know," Tanner said honestly.

"There's no telling," William said. "For all we know, your sister may be dead already."

Ella lunged forward, placing her hands on William's neck, and began to strangle him. He quickly fought his way out of her grasp and locked her head into his left arm, placing a knife at her throat. He shook and stumbled in his drunken state.

"Stop this, William! The prince wants her alive. It is your own life in danger now," Flesher yelled.

Tanner looked between the two men. Ella tried to break free, but William was too strong. Tanner knew that men are unrestrained when the bottle takes over their mind. And while they do not have much coordination, their strength is amplified.

The knife pressed harder against her skin. Ella tensed and closed her eyes. She was afraid her own efforts to break free were becoming dangerous. Suddenly Tanner rammed them both, sending them backward and then to the ground. A shocked, breathless Ella scrambled away from William, feeling her neck for injury. William lay on the ground under the point of Tanner's drawn sword. Flesher stepped forward also, so that two sharp swords now kept the drunkard on his back.

"Time for bed, William," Tanner reiterated.

William laughed a little. “You two are no fun.” He turned to Ella. “And you, well, I’ll have my way with you, sooner or later.”

Flesher volunteered to keep an eye on him until Ella had settled down for the night. Tanner hung the divider and prepared a place for her to sleep. Ella sat down on her blanket, hugging her knees. They were out of earshot of the others.

“Is this why you came for me? To take me to an evil prince whose designs you don’t know? And with dangerous escorts?”

Tanner squatted beside her. “Listen carefully to me, Ella,” he whispered. “I do not know what the prince is devising. I asked permission to try to find you because every night as I walked the halls of the kingdom castle, I heard your sister crying for you. She feared for your safety. I only wanted to help. It is my duty to help, because of my position, when I know that there is something amiss in the kingdom.” He waited for a reaction from Ella, but she only stared into the forest.

Tanner continued, “The prince never should have been involved. I will not take you to him until I know what he has planned. But I cannot take you back to Riverwood. It is in the opposite direction, and it is the first place William and Flesher will look for you. Is there somewhere else you can go to conceal yourself while I return to the castle alone?"

Ella knew of only one place. It was perfect. She knew they must be close to it already, and it was not too far from the castle by horse.

"Do you know Willow Top?" she asked.

"Willow Top? Yes, I know of Willow Top. Is there someplace there where you can stay?"

"There is my home, or where my home used to be. My mother and other sisters live there."

"Very good. Willow Top is situated between where we are now and the kingdom castle. I can escort you there and then carry on alone. I will tell your sister that you are well and discover what it is the prince wants with you. I will come back for you only if it is safe and truly necessary for you to see the prince."

"And what if it is not? You will leave me to guess? Am I to find my way back to Riverwood alone? It will be easy for me to hide at my mother's home; I may go entirely unnoticed. But I cannot bear it forever."

"Calm down, Ella." Her voice was beginning to rise, and Tanner feared the others would hear. He searched her eyes, regretting that it was too dark to see their hues of gold and green. "What is it about your home that puts you so ill at ease?"

"If you spent but two minutes there, you would see. Please don't just leave me there."

"Shhh now, or the others will hear. We'll have to be quiet. William will be as good as dead shortly. It is my night for guard. We need only wait until Flesher is asleep, and then we can go. I will escort you to Willow Top and your home. The kingdom castle will be a few short hours away. After I talk to your sister and learn of the prince's plans, I will come back for you. If it is safe to bring you to the castle, we will travel together. If it is not, I will return you to Riverwood. Is that pleasing to you?"

"None of this is pleasing to me! Riverwood holds the only happiness I have known for some time now. And you have taken me away."

Tanner couldn't help but feel guilty for causing her pain. The memories of Cinder's cries were nothing now to the girl suffering in front of him—the girl with the hair and eyes and spirit that he had grown very fond of. He tried to console her. "Think of your sister. She will be glad at least to know you are safe."

Thinking of Cinder caused Ella to remember what William had said. "Do you think it is really possible that she is dead?"

"All I know," Tanner spoke in a soft, soothing voice, "is that the prince is very dark. But I feel within me that your sister is safe. She has a grand reputation at the kingdom castle. She does excellent work."

"She's had lots of practice." Ella watched Tanner, wondering if she could trust him.

Tanner watched Ella, feeling remorse for having put her in danger. He had to keep her safe. Not because of his duty as a knight, but because she had, over the last few days, crawled up into his heart. "Try to get some rest. I will wake you when it is safe to go."

Ella lay down, and Tanner prepared Cassandra as if it were for the morning.

"You may rest, Flesher. I can take it from here."

Flesher made as comfortable a bed as possible. "She is a beautiful girl," he said before lying down. He looked at Tanner, a little wary.

"Yes, she is," Tanner remarked.

Neither of them spoke again.

When Flesher was breathing heavily, Tanner rose to his feet and cautiously walked around the divider. He watched Ella for a moment, granting her a little more rest, and then woke her with a gentle nudge. Ella was barely able to open her eyes and squinted, trying to see in the darkness.

"Cassandra is waiting for us. Let's go."

Tanner helped Ella to her feet. She wasn't able to walk well, being so stiff from the hard ground and days of horseback riding, so the knight lifted her in his arms and carried her. Ella woke up in time to help herself into the saddle. Tanner whispered to her as he led Cassandra quietly away from the camp. "We should reach Willow Top by morning."

11

Cinder loved her new position at the castle. Her studies in the mornings made her very learned and wise. She was sought after by many of her fellow servants for advice, help, and friendship. The prince continued to give her attention, inviting her to an occasional meeting or function, and Cinder grew fond of his steel-blue eyes and grand stature. There was also one thing that had become the pinnacle of her experience at the kingdom castle. Her new responsibilities came with the privilege of having access to the quarters of the king and queen and, occasionally, to the king and queen themselves.

"You do fine work, my dear," the queen would say.

"The castle has not been in such good shape for as long as I can remember," the king complimented.

All of this gave Cinder such satisfaction that going home became more and more difficult, especially now that she was allowed to go home for two days out of the week. She often stopped on her way at villages and points of interest. She became quite fond of a town by the name of Cobblestone. The homes had been around for such a long time that vines grew all around them. The people were friendly and, with the town being deep in a tangled wood, the air was pure and pleasant.

Only a few hours of each of her allotted days were actually spent at home. Cinder stayed long enough to give Katrina money for the week, play with Beatrice a little, and sit at her mother's side for a time.

One of these days, upon returning to the kingdom castle, Cinder found an invitation on her bed from the prince. It was beautifully handwritten in black and invited Cinder to be his guest at an upcoming ball. She was flattered beyond utterance. She held her excitement within but couldn't help producing a large smile. She returned her acceptance through a lesser servant, and Cinder quietly worked at her duties until the day of the ball with a secret gladness in her heart.

The sun had reached its highest point when Tanner and Ella finally stopped—well past morning. Tanner hopped down first. Ella reached down for him to lift her off, but the knight was distracted by the sound of hungry cries coming from the horse, and Ella slipped to the ground, landing on her hands and knees.

"I'm so sorry, miss." Tanner quickly reached down to help the maiden to her feet.

Ella pulled away from him and brushed off the front of her dress. "I fear it is you that wants my life—not the prince."

"Are you all right?" Tanner did not receive a reply to his question but rather a glare. "We must find a place for Cassandra to graze. Let's walk for a while."

The two were near the top of a steep hill. It reminded Ella of her family home. There were aspens in every direction. They were near a hollow that Ella could see if she stood in just the right spot. She could also hear a stream. It reminded her enough of everything that she loved—the good memories of her home, her adopted family, and the river—that she knew it would be difficult to leave.

"I thought you said we would be at Willow Top by morning." Tanner remained silent as he prepared to lead Cassandra to food and water. Ella watched him. "I'm not walking anywhere until you tell me how far we are." Tanner still did not answer. "You do know where we are, don't you?" Ella stood with fisted hands on her hips.

"Not exactly." His muffled voice was so soft that Ella barely heard him.

Ella did not know whether to yell at him or laugh at him. "I'm not going any farther with you until you figure out where it is that we are going."

Tanner's pride would not allow him to feel embarrassed. "Then I will be back soon. We were probably just a little farther away than I thought."

Ella ignored him as a smile crept up on her face.

"Are you sure you will be all right . . . staying here alone?" Tanner asked before leaving.

"I'll do my best not to get lost," Ella mocked. "Or rescued by any knights," she added as he began to walk away.

Ella was so glad to be alone. The sounds of the stream led her to it. Her steps were careful so her feet would be able to lead her back to the spot where she and Tanner had first stopped. A flat rock became her resting spot while she washed her hands, face, and feet. Sunshine burned into her hair and back.

The cool water was more than she could resist. She stepped into the stream and lowered herself until it came to her neck. It was the cleanest she had felt since first riding Cassandra.

Ella began to get cold after her wet hair and a cool breeze brushed against her neck at the same time. She rose to her feet and walked out of the stream. Her shoes dangled from one of her hands as she slowly retraced her steps. There was a clearing near where Cassandra had stood before Tanner led her off, where no trees kept the sun from warming the earth. Ella stretched out on the ground to rest and dry.

It was hours before Tanner returned. The sun was lower and Ella was now in the shade. The knight rode Cassandra, who carried a large cloth sling on each side of her. One was filled with firewood, and one carried a large, dead deer. The horse and knight came upon Ella, who, in her still-damp dress, lay upon the ground sleeping. Cassandra halted while Tanner quietly slid off the horse. He looked at the maiden to make sure he had not wakened her. Then he took the wood and deer down and started a fire. The smell of the cooking deer caused Ella to open her eyes.

She walked toward Tanner and the fire. "I'm glad to see that you found me again." Tanner did not look at Ella or answer her. She began to regret her words. "Are you angry with me . . . for teasing you?"

"No, miss. I do not imagine that anything you could do would make me angry."

Ella stood and watched him throw another log onto the fire. "I am grateful . . . that you took me away from the other two." Tanner was still quiet. "Even if you do seem to enjoy dropping me."

Tanner finally looked at Ella and smiled. Her arms were folded, and she was shivering. "You are wet, miss." Tanner walked to Cassandra and began fiddling with a few bags and straps. He pulled down the wool blanket and carried it to Ella.

"You may call me by my name if you would like," she said as he pulled the blanket tightly around her. She immediately felt the fire and the blanket working together to warm her.

Tanner could see the flames dancing in her eyes. "There you are . . . Ella."

"Are you going to push me over now?" Ella asked with a grin.

Tanner held up his hands and stepped back. "I won't even touch you."

Ella began walking around the fire and stumbled over a large pair of boots that had been placed in her path. There was no pride left in Tanner after that. He rushed to help her up but stumbled on first a rock and then a tree branch. Ella was on her feet before he was, and not only did she smile, but she had a hard time controlling her laughter.

Tanner moved his boots next to the tree where Cassandra was tied up; all the while Ella laughed at him. And though her hair and eyes had caught his attention and her spirit had won his affection, it was her smile and laugh that hooked him completely.

When the meat was cooked, Tanner prepared a portion for Ella on a plate of tree bark. "At least I brought you deer," he said as he handed it to her.

"You remembered?" Ella watched him get his own meat and sit down a few feet away from her.

"Of course I remembered."

"When do you suppose you'll remember where we are?" Ella began putting venison in her mouth to hide her smiles.

Tanner was beginning to find her teasing charming, even if it didn't help him to feel better about being so clumsy around her. He felt bad enough on his own at having been a constant, accidental hazard to her physical well-being.

"Wait a minute," Ella said as she sat up straight and looked to the top of the hill. "I know where we are." She stood up and looked in the direction of the glade she had seen earlier. She pointed as she spoke.

"Over there," she said. "Over there is Shepherd's Glade. I remember it from my geography lessons. It was at the base of a steep hill . . . on the other side of Willow Top. All we need to do is go to the other side of this mountain and we will be there."

Tanner considered her words. She could be right, but his pride had recovered a little. "You may be right, Ella. But the kingdom has a great deal of steep hills, and more than one glade."

Rather than argue, Ella continued to eat her supper.

There was no divider that night; they had left it in their hurry to flee from the prince's aides. Ella lay on one side of the fire, and Tanner on the other.

"Are you warm enough?" Tanner asked.

"I'll be all right." Ella's eyes were already closed, and the wool blanket was still wrapped tightly around her.

"I could keep the fire going."

Ella opened her eyes once more. "Thank you. That is a kind offer, but you need to get some sleep as well. You don't need to stay up and tend the fire. I will be warm enough under the blanket."

They both watched as the fire dimmed, and then they slept peacefully through the night.

12

Ella was up first—eager to prove she had been right about their location. Distant sounds of dogs and sheep told her they were indeed close to Shepherd's Glade. She had quickly grown fond of the place and would rather explore it than go home, but Tanner was beginning to rise.

"Over there are some berries to eat," she said as she folded her blanket and nodded toward a rock by the fire circle that held a bunch of red berries.

"Thank you," Tanner said as he sat up. He preferred watching her to eating, but he reached for the food.

When all of the supplies were loaded, and Cassandra had eaten some berries herself, Tanner and

Ella got up on the horse—by now Ella was skilled at lifting herself up—and their short journey began.

The top of the hill was not far away to a horse as strong as Cassandra and to two willing riders. Ella now sat upright with confidence, facing the front, leaning into Tanner slightly to allow him sight, and merely resting her hands on Cassandra's neck rather than pulling at her mane. She trusted Tanner to lead the horse without allowing her to fall, but she had decided that from now on she would be getting herself down rather than risk breaking her neck.

They reached the top, and Ella began to fear that she was not where she had thought. She turned to look behind her, and Shepherd's Glade was now in clear sight. It was even more beautiful from the top than from the small corner view of it she had spotted before. "I don't understand," she began. She slid off of the horse and tried to look more carefully at her surroundings. "There's Shepherd's Glade, and I can almost see the top of my mother's house, but where . . . ?"

Ella turned to look at the spot where her father's favorite tree had once been. She became furious as she beheld a stump with fresh splinters and ax markings. She turned to Tanner, her face glowering and red. "Where did you get that firewood?"

Tanner raised his eyebrows. The look on Ella's face was frightening.

"I believe I got it from right here, miss—I mean, Ella."

Ella knelt next to the tree stump. "Who chops down a willow tree for firewood?" She was trying not to cry, knowing it wouldn't help, but it was her father's tree—the one hope in all of these years that her father might still be alive.

"It was old, miss. And beginning to dry out. I believe willow burns better than aspen, anyway." Tanner was shocked at the whole picture and not sure what to do. "Have I done something to offend you, Ella? Was this tree important to you?"

She turned to him and snapped, "It was my father's tree!"

The poor knight was even more confused. "Is your father dead?" Why else would she be so upset?

"He is now!"

Tanner began to understand. "The legend? You know of the legend of the trees? Is that what you mean?"

Ella looked at him, trying to compose herself. "Of course I know about the legend of the trees. Why wouldn't I?" Her calmer voice encouraged Tanner to keep talking.

"It's just that the legend of the trees is something that is taught at the kingdom castle. Many people in the kingdom don't know of it. Unless you have been there—"

"My father told me from the time I was a small child." Ella wondered if her father had learned it at the castle. He had never told her where he had heard it, and as far as Ella knew, he had never been to the castle before.

Tanner spoke again. "The legend says that each human on the earth has a tree to care for, and that a person's tree will also care for him or her. As long as the tree is thriving, the person will live, and as long as the person is living well, the tree will survive. Is this what you are speaking of?"

"It sounds like what my father told me."

"And he said that this was his tree?"

"Yes."

Tanner felt horrible. Whether the legend was true or not, Ella obviously believed it. He sat on the ground, and Ella sat next to him. The patient knight asked her to tell him all about her father and his tree. Ella told him everything: how her father had disappeared, how her family treated her and each other, how Cinder had gone to work at the castle, and how the willow was the one hope of her father's existence.

When the story was finished, Ella could see the despair in the knight's face. She began to feel sorry for having been so harsh with him when his act had been only an accident. She leaned toward him and softly kissed his cheek. Then she rose to her feet and began walking down the hill toward the cottage where she had once lived. Tanner followed, pulling Cassandra along behind him, and couldn't help but smile as he placed his hand to the cheek where he had just felt her lips.

Ella hesitated when they reached the cottage.

"Would you like me to come in with you?"

Ella looked at the knight. She had grown fond of him and his company. She feared that if he came inside, he would . . . not want to come back.

She gave him a brave smile. "I'll manage. You should ride on to the castle."

Tanner did not want to leave. He bent toward her and kissed her on the forehead.

"I care for you, Ella. More than I should as a knight. I think of you as more than a maiden whom it is my duty to protect. I will come back for you, one way or another."

The words came as a surprise to Ella. "Are you . . . ? Are you telling the truth? Do you really care for me?"

He cupped a hand on her firm jaw. "Is it so hard to believe?"

Ella looked to the ground. She had lost herself before—once in her own home, and now possibly the part of her that belonged in Riverwood was gone as well. Did she really belong with a knight from the kingdom castle that she barely knew?

Tanner lifted her delicate chin until she was looking at him again. "Yes. I care for you. I promise I won't leave you here for long."

Ella burrowed deeply into his chest and wrapped her arms around his waist.

Now it was Tanner's turn to be surprised. He kissed the top of her head, savoring the moment until he remembered the urgency of their situation. Having been lost for a day, they had little time. Flesher and William were surely close behind them. "I really should get going."

Ella held on tighter for a moment. She couldn't say why, but being with him was different than anything she had ever felt before. It was calming and natural, like when the wind comes at exactly the right moment to dispell the heat of the sun.

He kissed her on the top of her head one more time, and Ella let go.

Tanner turned to mount Cassandra, glanced one last time at Ella, then rode down the hill, around a corner, and out of sight.

Ella turned, and as she looked at the house, all of the wonder and excitement of the moment before vanished.

13

The cries began even before the door was completely open.

"Is that Cinderella?" Mother asked Katrina.

Katrina stared at Ella, then with a nasty look on her face said, "No, Mother. It is some strange girl. I've never seen her before."

"Well, what does she want?"

Ella looked around the room. An array of furniture acted as a wall, barricading the mother into a corner. The wall's purpose became obvious when Beatrice came into the room and threw a large clay pitcher through the air. It crashed on the wall by the stairs.

"She has come to clean up after Beatrice, Mother," Katrina said as she fixed her long, dark hair in the mirror. This appeased the mother, and she did not speak of it again.

There were several more mirrors on the walls than there had been before, and most of them were broken. Katrina was wearing a dress that looked fit for a queen. Ella was already angry, knowing that Katrina was throwing Cinder's hard-earned money away on fancy clothes and mirrors that acted as shooting targets. Beatrice threw a spoon, which hit Ella on the corner of her eye, causing a slow trickle of blood to slide down her face.

Ella quickly swept up the pitcher. Then she took the spoon and bent it around Beatrice's arm so that it was stuck. The child wailed, but Ella ignored her and walked up the stairs.

"I'm going out soon," Katrina yelled up after her, "with a handsome boy from the village. You'll have to do everything else for the rest of the day."

Ella ignored her too. She hated being in the house. She entered her old room and thought of all the nights she and Cinder had spent in travail because of the family troubles, and of even earlier years when the four sisters had played games together. They would pull a mattress from Katrina's room—back then it had belonged to Katrina and Cinder—and jump from the bed to the mattress on the floor. Ella closed the door and propped a chair against it just under the doorknob to prevent anyone from coming in. Then she sat on her bed and watched and waited.

It was the day of the ball, and Cinder had worked extra hard to complete all her tasks by early afternoon. She had succeeded and even helped a few other servants with their duties so that they could help her get ready. The dark green velvet dress had been purchased by Cinder's endless hard work. It was simple, but its simplicity made it even more appealing. It had a high waist, and the top was trimmed with cream lace. The long sleeves and hem of the dress were lined in the same way. She wore her hair up, with a few cascading curls framing her face.

The plain girl, turned servant, turned honored guest of the prince, was picturesque as she walked down the corridors. But it only took a few seconds in the grand ballroom for Cinder to feel utterly out of place. It was as if every pair of eyes was staring at her. Her dress was quite plain compared to those of the other girls, which were scarlet and purple with frills, jewels, and layers of fancy fabric. She was a single pearl sitting among mountains of diamonds and gold.

She considered turning to leave before she became the object of ridicule, but her thoughts left her as soon as she saw the prince. His dark hair, olive skin, wide eyes, and pleasant face captured her attention. He motioned for her to come to him. Confidence was Cinder's newfound friend from that moment on. She sat beside him at a long and sturdy table. Couples were dancing. Others were eating. And some sat in chairs lining the walls, chatting happily. For the first time in her life, Cinder was among the clouds.

Tanner reached the castle at sundown. The full moon was already peeking over the distant hills. He left his horse at the stables, and then the good knight ran to the castle to find Lord Tracey.

Tanner barged into the same meeting room where he had encountered the lord before, only this time a meeting was in session.

Lord Tracey was not pleased by Tanner's forceful intrusion. "Where have you put the girl? And where are the others?"

Tanner ignored Lord Tracey's questions as well as the other dozen pair of eyes that were staring at him. "I need to speak with the prince," he said.

"The prince is at the ball. And it may take weeks to get you an appointment with his majesty."

"That won't do. I need to speak with the prince right away. I need to know what his intentions are concerning the girl."

Tracey's face became grim as he spoke to Tanner in hushed, dark tones. "It is not your place, knight, to question the prince. Now what have you done with the girl?"

Tanner did not lower his voice even though there was an audience for what should have been a private conversation. "The girl is waiting for me in a safe place. I left the prince's drunk, cowardly, poor excuses for companions along the road home. I would guess that they are either at the bottom of a lake or at the bottom of a very dry bottle. Now, I must speak to the prince immediately."

"You fool! How dare you speak to me like that when you have put all of our lives in danger? If the prince is displeased, it will be not only their lives, but yours and mine as well. I highly recommend that you locate the girl as well as the others if you have any wish to live."

The low advisor's sharp words did not deter the brave knight. He marched straight to the grand ballroom, where he easily spotted Prince Monticello at the center of the great table, the lovely gray-haired maiden at his side.

"Have you had any news of my sister?" Cinder asked the prince.

"No, I have not yet, but I am expecting them any day, maybe even tonight."

Tanner walked toward them with fast, determined steps, even as the prince was finishing his sentence. He was as the dung among all of the beautiful garden flowers and quickly became the center of everyone's attention. The prince gave a glance to one of his aides. The aide stood and addressed Sir Tanner.

"Good knight, you must take your matter to one of the low advisors. That is the law, and as you can see, we are in the middle of a gay ball and do not wish for any adverse news."

"I will speak to the prince before I leave the room." Tanner stared at a spot on the wall, his wide nose raised slightly and his arms clasped behind his back.

Even though it was apparent that Tanner was quite serious, the prince's aide snickered and then motioned for the two knights guarding the doors to escort their brother from the room.

"Wait!" called the prince. He did not want Cinder knowing that he was a cold and cruel being. "You have been on a long journey. Come, eat with us and . . ." Prince Monticello looked over his unkempt appearance, "refresh yourself."

"No, your majesty. I only wish to discuss a crucial matter with you." Tanner looked into the prince's calm eyes, wanting only to show that he had no fear of his cruelty and evil.

"Crucial?" the prince scoffed.

"Well, maybe not to you. I have come to discuss your intentions with a maiden named Ella, whose sister is seated beside you. But I think perhaps you are too unfeeling to care."

Cinder looked at the prince. Having been so enthralled by the evening, she only then recognized Tanner as the knight who had first inquired about her sister.

"Ella? Do you have news of Ella?" Cinder stood up from her chair and began walking toward Sir Tanner.

"No, Cinder, there is as yet no news of your sister." The prince stood also, holding out a hand to beckon her to come back to her seat.

Cinder turned to face the prince. "But he says he has news. Please hear it. I know you are too good to make me wait until after the ball to discuss my sister Ella."

The prince was always careful not to be caught in one of his lies, but this time he had come close. There were too many knights in the kingdom to keep track of them all, and until that moment, Monticello had not realized that the knight standing before him was the knight he had been waiting for.

Monticello walked to Cinder and whispered in her ear. "I will go and hear what he has to say and then bring the news to you. I won't allow him to spoil your evening any further." He stroked her soft, round cheek and nudged her toward her seat at the table. "Sit back down, Cinder. This is a ball. And you are supposed to be having a good time." Once Cinder was seated again, with a look of anxious concern on her face, the prince walked toward Tanner and motioned for Tanner to follow him outside the ballroom.

The prince listened as Tanner explained how he'd left William and Flesher alone in the forest, and then he had the knight imprisoned for kidnapping. Prince Monticello returned to the ball and informed Cinder of everything. Then he took a weeping, worried maiden back to his quarters.

"I don't understand, sir. He told you that my sister is dead, but you don't believe him?"

"No, I certainly do not believe him. You see, he was promised a reward for returning by the full moon. I am sure that he gave up on finding your sister and returned with a lie in order to obtain his prize. I will send another expedition for her, and this time I will be going myself."

Cinder looked up at the prince with a gleam of hope in her eyes, which were still moist. "Will you really?"

"My dear Cinder . . ." He walked toward her, placed both of his large hands on her face, and looked into her eyes as though he cared greatly for her. "Of course I will. You had better get back to your room. I will leave first thing in the morning."

Cinder lingered until Prince Monticello removed his hands from her face. As she turned to leave, the prince said, "I am sorry about the ball. When I come back, I will have another, and you will again sit at my side."

The prince's intense gaze and mesmerizing smile caused Cinder to almost forget about the news of Ella. She smiled at him, knowing she would not soon get those eyes out of her head. "You are too good, sir. Thank you." She gave him one last glance before leaving him alone.

In prison, Tanner protested with such passion—not to mention the occasional outburst of irritating song—that the prison guard finally sent for Lord Tracey by Tanner's request.

"In prison, I see? And I'll be next, I suppose. It serves you right." Lord Tracey said upon seeing Tanner. He turned to leave.

"Lord Tracey! Do you know any of the prince's dark secrets?" Tanner gripped the prison bars firmly, and the lord could feel the knight's eyes burning into his back.

Lord Tracey halted.

"Please don't pretend to be ignorant of the cunning, deceit, and pure evil that the prince has produced in this kingdom. You have witnessed it. You have allowed it. You have been a part of it."

The low advisor waited but did not turn around to face the accusations.

"Will you please investigate the two girls who are dependent upon us to help them? Something is not right. It involves a servant girl in the kingdom castle, with hair the color of the ashes in the fire circle when the fire is long out. It involves her sister, a virtuous and fair maiden who deserves nothing but goodness. And it involves a prince, one that we are both unfortunately acquainted with, and whose evil knows no bounds."

Lord Tracey looked at Tanner, but only over his shoulder. His black robe reached to the ground, and with the dark gray stone of the walls behind him, his face was a circle of light among all the blackness.

"Do you know what the prince keeps in the tower above his quarters?"

"No," Tanner said with curiosity and suspicion.

"Do you know where the two girls of whom you speak are from?"

"Yes. Ella and Cinder both used to live in Willow Top."

"Then you know half of this dark secret. I'm afraid I can't help you, except maybe in pleading your case when the prince considers whether to let you go or hang you. Please don't misunderstand me. It's not that I don't care about these girls. It's just that nothing can be done." Lord Tracey, too unfeeling to give further help, eyed Tanner for a moment and then turned to leave.

Tanner was left to stew over the words of the king's low advisor. They did not make any sense to him. He smacked the wall with his hand. There was no hope of escape, and the beautiful maiden that he was in love with would be waiting for a man that would never come.

14

Ella lay restless that night. Beatrice's horrible fits had frayed each of her nerves one by one. Her younger sister had fallen asleep while banging from the inside of their bedroom door, trying to get their mother's attention since Ella would give her none, but by that time, the damage had been done.

Katrina was still not home. Ella began to feel a darkness seep into the room and her soul. She did not feel well, and the only thought that calmed her was the thought of going to the castle to find Tanner.

She got out of bed, pushed aside Beatrice who was still in front of the door, and went downstairs. Her mother was still spinning.

"Mother?" There was no answer. "Mother, I am going to the kingdom castle."

"My daughter Cinderella works at the kingdom castle. I am so proud of her." She stopped for a moment to readjust the wool.

That was not the encouragement that Ella had so foolishly wished for at the start of such an expedition. She changed into some of her father's old clothes and pulled back her long hair as a disguise. Then she snuck into the kitchen to get a knife for protection. Thus her journey to the castle began.

She walked slowly while it was still dark. Ella had lived in a dark wood all her life, but somehow walking in them this night made her uneasy. Every call of a bird or wisp of wind frightened her. Even the sound of crickets, which usually calmed her while she lay in bed, was now eerie and unwelcome. Crickets could not save her if danger found her, and she would have preferred silence.

The time seemed endless before the sun began to rise, but then the sky took on a glow followed by an array of pinks, yellows, and blues, like a girl who cannot decide what dress to wear. In the light, Ella found her courage again and her walk became rapid. She even ran some of the distance.

Several carriages passed her on the road, but none stopped to offer assistance. Ella didn't mind, for she knew that for every one that might be of help, there might also be one that brought trouble. She had never been to the kingdom castle before, and she wondered if the road to it was always this busy or if some days it sat without population.

The berries she ate on the way did not give sufficient strength, and she did not reach the castle before sunset as she had wished. But just before the sun blew out its last candle and gave way to the dark of night, Ella saw the tallest tower. More of the structure was visible with every step as the trees thinned and the castle grounds began to open before her.

Never had she imagined it was so grand—each tower pointing heavenward, topped with great, waving flags that bore the crest of the king. There was one large door in the center of the castle. She counted the windows, and, when she lost count, started again. Thirty-seven of them glowed with candlelight, but there could have been more that she did not see in the darkness. The castle was on a hill, and while the trees had thinned, there were still many clusters of them that grew tall around the structure.

The moon was beginning to rise over the mountains in the distance. Ella noticed the crest of the king once more as she passed through the entrance gate. She reached her hand to touch it, remembering when she first saw it on the horses outside the Robinsons' home.

The king's tree was the greatest in the kingdom. It was said to be strong, pure white, and indestructible. *But it is only a legend*, Ella reminded herself. She forced herself to believe it. Because if the legend was true, then surely her father was dead, now that his tree had been chopped down.

Ella walked up a path that was made of stone, unlike the dirt roads and pathways in the remainder of the kingdom. A line of knights stood on either side of the path, each perhaps fifteen feet apart. Their arms were at their sides when she entered the gate, but as she passed by each set of knights standing across from one another, they would in unison move their hands to their swords in warning. Ella watched them carefully as she passed. She had never seen Tanner in his full armor. It was intimidating, as if they were creatures rather than men. Could his eyes be inside one of those helmets—watching but unable to make his presence known?

Four armored knights stood guard at the front of the kingdom castle wall, along with one man who was dressed in only clothing—but clothing much finer than Ella had ever seen in Willow Top or Riverwood. A gold pattern on his robe seemed to shine under the blazing firelight coming from two granite bowls perched on pillars almost as tall as Ella that stood on either side of the entrance.

Even in men's clothing, Ella easily passed for a maiden in need and was granted access to the servants' quarters. She explained that her family was in crisis and that her sister was needed. The robed man knew of Cinder and seemed to give Ella a bit more respect after hearing her name, although he continued to look questionably at her appearance.

One of the knights led her inside. The halls were wide, and the ceilings seemed to reach as high as mountains do. The servants' quarters were not far from the entrance, and Ella was passed on to another knight who walked their corridors. He knew of the girl with the gray hair and took Ella straight to Cinder's small room.

The knights in the castle walked about with less armor than the knights outside—much like Tanner had been dressed when they first met. The knight she followed had no helmet and from the back reminded her of William, with curly hair and a bit of stoutness. Before he knocked on the door, Ella asked him if he knew a knight by the name of Tanner.

"Of course I know Tanner. He used to be stationed here in the servants' quarters with me." The knight leaned closer to Ella and whispered, "He is in prison now."

Ella gasped. "Prison? For what?"

"Prince Monticello had him put in prison for kidnapping." The knight's face darkened, and he leaned even closer to whisper even softer. "But I know Tanner. And he wouldn't do that. The prince is up to something, if you ask me. I don't know who Tanner is accused of kidnapping, but it must have been someone important to the prince."

Those words caused all of Ella's blood to chill. What did the prince want with her? And why was it so important that he would put Tanner in prison for not bringing her back? "After I speak to my sister, would it be possible for you to take me to him?"

The knight looked behind him and around the hallway. He returned to Ella and whispered close to her again. "Yes, it would be possible. Risky—only those who work at the castle are allowed in the dungeons—but possible."

"Will you take me?" Her wide, worried eyes pleaded fiercely. He would take her, or she would find her own way there.

"I will supply you with some armor and show you the way, but beyond that, there is nothing that I can do to help you." The knight turned to knock on Cinder's door.

Ella waited, greatly troubled by the new information. She rubbed her hands nervously while she and the knight waited for Cinder to answer.

Cinder came shortly. She held a lighted candlestick, and her eyes were squinted. Her silver hair was pulled into a braid, but several strands were displaced, and she held a thin, light blue robe tightly around her nightdress. When her eyes had adjusted, she threw her arms around Ella in joyous disbelief, dripping a few drops of hot wax in Ella's hair. "Ella, you are safe! I knew the prince would find you."

"The prince?" Ella pulled herself out of her sister's arms. "Cinder, I came here on my own. I've never met the prince, and I am sure that I do not want to." She looked her sister in the eye but continued to hold onto her arms.

"Don't say such things, Ella. I am in love with the prince." Cinder covered her mouth after saying it. She glanced at the knight, who was standing against the wall, still very close to the door. If he had heard, his face did not show it.

Ella released her sister. Nothing could have prepared her for this news. "The prince is evil, Cinder."

In the next moment, Cinder came as close to snapping as she ever had before. "How would you know that?" She looked at Ella from the top of her head all the way down to her feet and back again. "You've been off hiding in your own self-pity and selfish ways. You left me alone to care for the family. I've been here working for them, and I've been educated. The prince is good and noble indeed. Every day I learn of some good thing that the prince has done. This very day he told me that he would go looking for you since that scheming knight came back without you."

"The prince was coming for me?" Ella's frustration with her sister was turning into fear. What did he want with her?

"He said he would leave in the morning, but he must have left after we spoke since you are already here."

Now Ella sounded like the older of the two. "Cinder, I told you, I came here myself. If the prince is after me, then I must be in danger. And you may be also."

Cinder laughed at her sister. "The prince would never hurt me. I have a high station here at the castle. My work is famous. Besides, I think that the prince may be falling in love with me." This time she had spoken softly enough to prevent the knight from hearing.

Ella wanted to argue with her sister, but she knew she had already wasted enough time. "I'm sure you're right, Cinder. I can see you are well enough without me. I will go back to my selfish ways. I wish you well."

Ella turned to leave and waited for the knight to lead her away. Only then did Cinder begin to feel remorse for her words. All this time, she had been in such despair because she had worried for Ella, and rather than hold onto her, she had pushed her away.

Ella and the knight were out of sight now. Cinder was tormented because she had opened her mouth and let words slip out that she ought to have kept inside. And now she could not call those words back from Ella's memory.

15

The knight covered Ella in full armor and gave her simple directions to the prison. She was advised to keep her helmet on so as not to draw attention from the guard. Ella walked down a steep spiral staircase until she was well below the level of the earth. There were several cells on this floor and all of them were full, but there was no sign of Tanner. There was another staircase across the circular room. Ella descended it until she reached the lowest level of the prison dungeons. Tanner was lying on the hard, stone floor with his eyes open. Ella stood in front of his cell watching him.

Tanner did not move anything but his lips. "Leave me be."

Ella stood still.

Tanner got to his feet and walked to the bars that stood between him and the girl who was dressed as a knight. He whispered, "Unless you have come to rescue me, I beg you to leave me alone here."

"Tanner . . ." The feeling in Ella's voice surprised even her.

Tanner's eyebrows rose as a hopeful expression came to his face. "Ella, is that you in there?" Tanner placed his hands on the bars and looked as though he was trying to get his head in between them.

"Yes. I'm so sorry. It hurts me to see you in prison, especially when it is my fault." Ella may have wanted to slump and cry, but somehow, as the armor forced her to stand upright, it also made the idea of crying ridiculous.

"It isn't your fault, Ella. Don't say that." Tanner awkwardly tried to reach out to her through the bars. It was lucky there were no guards and the other cells on the level were empty, since the sight of a knight without armor trying to hug a knight with armor surely would have been suspicious.

Ella held onto the bars as well. "Well, there is one good thing about you being in prison. I just realized that while you're in there, you certainly cannot do anything to hurt me, so I will not be trying to rescue you."

Tanner let out a breath of laughter before turning serious. "Ella, I have learned something about why the prince is looking for you, although I do not understand it."

"What is it?" Ella asked earnestly.

Tanner whispered low, "It has to do with something that the prince is keeping in the tower above his chambers. One of the king's low advisors mentioned it to me, but he wouldn't tell me anything else about it."

"How do I get there?" She pulled away from the bars, resolved to be on her way.

Tanner tightened his grip on the bars, as if trying to shake his way free. "Ella, I won't let you go. It is too dangerous." He could not see the smile forming on her lips.

"And how exactly were you planning to stop me?"

He bowed his head and rested it on the prison bars. "Please, Ella. Don't go looking for danger."

She lowered her head to his and whispered slowly. "Sometimes, things come to you whether you go looking for them or not—danger, disaster . . . love." Ella freed her right hand of its armor and placed her cold palm on the side of Tanner's face. "Please tell me where the prince's chamber is."

"You know you're torturing me. You tell me that you love me and then ask me to help you find your way to a place where someone or something may be waiting to harm you." He glared at her, a feigned anger emanating from his face and eyes.

"I didn't say that I love you, I only pointed out the fact that sometimes things happen whether you go looking for them or not."

It was so easy for Ella to charm, even through thick armor. Tanner was falling for her even deeper than he had before.

"Could you really love such a clumsy knight?"

It was now insecurity, longing, and hope that came from his face, and it made Ella nervous. She closed her eyes so she could not see his face and would be able to concentrate. "Could I? Would I?" She acted as though she was truly thinking about it.

Her teasing only added to the knight's afflictions. "Do you?"

Ella finally became serious, and she opened her eyes once again, although Tanner was not able to really see them. "Yes, I'm afraid I do."

Tanner looked at her intently.

"But I'm also afraid that I still want you to tell me where I can find the tower." It made her feel good and gave her confidence to see the true concern in his eyes.

Tanner sighed in resignation and then whispered lower than he had in their conversation thus far. "Leave the prison dungeons and go to the south end of the castle. There are three corridors. The prince resides at the end of the middle corridor. To the side of his door is a staircase. It will lead you to the tower."

Ella closed her eyes and retraced her entrance through and movements about the castle. She had been a bit turned around inside, but when she thought it out, she knew which way was south.

"Please be careful. I can only imagine what horrible things he keeps behind locked doors."

"How am I to get in if the door is locked?"

"Your sister must have a key. You will have to get it from her, either by persuasion or theft."

Ella smiled. "What would I do without you?"

The answer to that question saddened the shameful knight. "You'd be safe in Riverwood, without any of this trouble or worry, remember?"

"Oh, right. Remind me again why I love you."

Tanner's anxiety over her was escalating, and as much as he wanted her to stay, he mostly wanted her to have already returned safely. "Go now. Come back and tell me what you discover."

Ella turned to go, and Tanner smiled as he watched her try to walk in a full suit of armor.

"Come back," he whispered to himself after she disappeared up the spiral staircase.

16

Ella walked freely about the castle and was glad to see that a few of the castle knights did have full armor on. She had begun to feel conspicuous among the knights who wore tunics over chain armor rather than a full breastplate. Many of the knights in full armor carried their helmets in their hands, but a few still wore them over their heads, and Ella was grateful that she could blend in somewhat. She returned to the servants' quarters where the same knight who took her to Tanner still guarded the hallways. He allowed Ella access to her sister's room. Ella was not about to wake her sister and risk another confrontation. Quietly, she searched the room for a key. The problem was not finding where the key was kept, but determining which key she needed, since there was a stash of nearly one hundred keys on about fifteen different rings. But since all the rings were kept in a single basket, Ella simply lifted the whole basket and walked out the door.

The lighting dimmed until Ella reached the middle corridor, and then it disappeared altogether. Blindly, she walked down the hallway. It was longer than she had anticipated, and she found herself taking each step with caution to avoid walking straight into the prince's door.

It was silent except for her own breathing inside the helmet she wore. Ella reached out one hand in front of her to feel her way. Her other arm cradled the basket full of keys. At last, she felt a large wooden door. Her fingers ran across the door until she reached a stone wall again. Knowing she had chosen the wrong side of the door, Ella turned around. Now that her eyes had adjusted and she was looking in the right direction, she could see something. A small hallway led to a spiral staircase, and she could see the first few stairs. A strange combination of relief and horror filled her breast. She walked slowly to and up the staircase. Higher and higher she went until she entered a small circular room with a single door. There was a tiny window looking out over the grounds behind the castle. The moonlight coming in through the window was the only thing allowing her sight.

It was difficult for Ella to kneel in front of the door while fully dressed as a knight. She held onto the lock with her left hand and used her right to try every key, setting aside each ring after she was through with it. After a while, she learned that only the keys with two thin, jagged protrusions fit into the hole. This sped up the process of sorting through them. Soon, she was merely setting aside all of the key rings except those that contained a key with that certain quality. When she was finished, there were only three rings and ten keys left. Her hands began to shake and her heart beat quickly and heavily. It was thrilling to be down to the last key, but it too failed in opening the door.

"May I help you?" a sinister voice asked.

Ella hadn't noticed the dim light of a candle glowing behind her. She stumbled and dropped the last of the keys she had been trying. The sounds of her armor clanging against the wall and of the keys being shifted around echoed loudly in the stillness.

"I didn't mean to frighten you, my good knight. But surely you must know the punishment for such an act as trying to break into the prince's private quarters."

She didn't want to speak. Ella rose to her feet.

The prince took in the sight before him—oversized armor, no sword. "You are very small for a knight." Prince Monticello reached his hand forward and pulled the helmet off of her and then leaned back to get a good look. "Ella of Willow Top, I was just coming to see you."

Ella spoke calmly and softly. "What do you want with me, villain?"

"The crimes are piling up. First breaking into the castle, then trying to break into my room, and now calling me names. And your sister is your accomplice. She'll have to be punished too."

The calmness left Ella. "My sister did nothing wrong. I broke into her chamber and stole the keys myself."

"Ella, who knew you were so devious?" He glared at her, all the while with a wicked smile on his face. "I could let you in. It would be a shame for you to come this far and break so many laws for nothing. Shall we?"

The prince walked to the door and pulled a key from inside his long hooded cloak. He unlocked the door and pushed it open slightly. The light from the top of the staircase made its way inside the room, casting a tall, thin ray onto the stone floor.

"You're not going to make me go in alone, are you?" he asked as he looked back at her.

There was something about the prince that would have made Ella avoid ever going anywhere with him, but did she really have a choice? "What are you hiding in there?"

"Come in. I will show you." His black hair fell over his forehead and covered half of his ears. She could see why Cinder had fallen for him. His evil was masked behind charming features. But he would not fool Ella.

Ella took a few hesitant steps toward him and through the door. The prince closed it behind her. The temperature dropped to a winter cold, and she shivered—partly because of the cold and partly because of her fear. The candle didn't give enough light to see what was in the room, but she heard a few muffled coughs and moans and saw some lumpy shapes that she couldn't distinguish.

"Just let me get the curtains," the prince said in a sing-song voice. Ella could hear him walk away from her, and then the silver rings attached to the dark curtains scraped across the metal bar that held them up, first one side followed by the other.

The light of the night sky filled the room, which Ella could now see was the shape of the moon when it is little more than a sliver. In the center of the room sat a being. A few others were scattered about—all resting on the floor, all dirty, and all motionless. They were also all chained. Ella became a statue, focusing on the man in the center of the crescent-shaped room.

"Don't you recognize him? I was expecting quite the reunion from you." The innocent look on the prince's face would have infuriated Ella, but she was not looking at him.

"Father?" Ella began to cry as she ran and knelt at her father's side. She clasped his limp arm and tried to hug it despite her armor-covered body. "Father, what has he done to you?" Ella turned to the prince. "Is this a prison?"

"No, this is not a prison." He spoke to Ella as if she was very foolish. "He has everything he needs to escape. This, my dear, is merely an experiment. The lock on the door is to keep people out, and the key to the chains is on his person. He could leave if he wanted."

"Father, is this true? Do you stay here in this tower of your own accord?"

Her father did not answer her. He was sitting with his knees to his chest. His hair had grown long and now covered his face, which was tan, not from the sun, but from years of dirt and neglect.

Ella felt her father's clothing until she located the key in the pocket of his pants. She tried to get to it, but her father resisted. He pulled away from her, covered the pocket with his hands, and pushed her away until she fell onto her back side. His physical strength was no match for hers, but he fought with such determination that Ella could not succeed.

Anger began to overshadow her sadness. She forced the tears to stop. "What evil game are you playing, sir?" Ella's voice was darker than any moonless night sky had ever been.

"I do not play games, Ella. I simply experiment. Your father was a willing subject. At least, he did not protest much. It was quite easy to lead him here. And as you can see, he stays. Actually, I had a good hold upon his mind even before he came to the castle." He stood with his hands clasped behind his back.

His calmness and pitiless manner caused Ella's anger to spike. She yelled with fury. "How can you so easily discharge such lies? You tell me he stays here of his own accord, and in the same breath you tell me that you have control of his mind."

Prince Monticello leaned back with his arms folded and spoke as coolly as an early spring breeze. "Don't get so upset, Ella. He does love you so, or at least he used to."

She turned away from the prince once more. "Father! Father, it's me, Ella!" Ella held onto his cold arm and shook as she yelled, the links of the chains sounding in the dimness. "Don't you remember, Father? Remember Mother? Cinder and Katrina and Beatrice? Father, you must remember! Don't you care for us anymore?" Ella choked back the tears that were trying to find their way out of her.

"I tried the rest of you too, you know. I thought maybe you had been weakened when he disappeared. I haven't had any success yet. But I am not one to give up easily."

At this point, Ella wanted nothing more than to keep him talking. "What is it that you want with me, Prince Monticello?" Her hunched-over body was secretly at work trying to reach the knife that she had hidden underneath her layers of armor and clothing.

"I just wanted you to see your father. Isn't that what you've been looking for all these years? And I have brought you here. I have answered all of those wishes you made into the sky out your window."

Ella paused while the prince began to walk around her and her father.

"He used to love all of you. It was very difficult to get you in particular out of his mind, though. Parents really shouldn't have favorites; your sisters must hate you. But eventually I was able to convince him that you were all rather . . . disappointing."

His arms were still folded, and he seemed unaware of Ella's scrambling.

Ella had a tight hold on the knife and a mad look in her eye. The prince was still talking, but Ella no longer needed or wanted an explanation. She only wanted one thing. And as the prince looked down at her with no penitence, Ella jumped in his direction and stabbed him in the heart.

17

Prince Monticello looked shocked for a moment and then began to laugh.

"You can't kill me, Ella," he said as he pulled the knife from his chest.

There was no blood, no pain, and Prince Monticello turned to leave, a stunned Ella staring after him.

The prince's fading footsteps were the only sound now, and as he walked away, he spoke. "By the way, I'm still locking up your sister."

Ella listened to him descend the stairs, and then there was silence. She was now alone with her father and the other lifeless souls. Weston's eyes were heavy and enlarged. The clothing he wore was shredded. Filth covered his skin. His hair was pulled back with a scrap of cloth from his shirt. He had aged decades since Ella last saw him. The once spry, handsome father she knew had become an old man—sick and troubled.

"Father? Father, I can see you. Where are you?" She began pulling on his arm, trying to get him up. When that didn't work, she grabbed his other arm and pulled with all of her might. The armor was getting in her way, and she cried out in frustration.

He never even looked at her.

Rage and wrath pulled Ella's heart away from her father's side. She replaced the helmet, retrieved the knife that the prince had dropped to the floor, and ran down the stairs and back through the dark hallway. She turned the corner at the intersection. The halls were now lit with fire. She spun around when she did not see Prince Monticello in one direction, and there was his swaying black cloak, getting smaller and smaller with each passing second.

Ella ran down the hallway and lunged for him. She stabbed him again, exactly where she thought his heart must have been, and then pulled the knife back out. The glint of fear in his eyes when he turned around encouraged Ella, and she stabbed him twice more in the front. The prince never even made a sound. He did not fall to the floor or try to stop her.

He grabbed her wrist tight, and Ella had no choice but to drop the knife. "I told you, Ella. You cannot kill me. I was just on my way to get your sister. Would you like to see her off to the dungeon?"

Ella tried to break free from his hold. "I told you that my sister is innocent. If you must lock somebody up, then let it be me."

The prince's voice had escalated, and now there was no disguising his anger. "No, I think you'll suffer more in freedom while everything you love is bound."

Ella thought of Tanner for the first time since she had reached the prince's dark corridor. Could the prince read her thoughts? Did he know Tanner was included in that category?

The prince spoke as Ella followed him to the servants' quarters. "I've been good to Cinder, but that ends now. And there is nothing you can do to stop me from hurting her."

"She'll never believe you!"

Prince Monticello laughed and then stopped his rapid pace to face Ella. "Remember who you're talking to. Remember how easy it was for me to ensnare your father. Do not underestimate my power. Cinder already trusts me. I know it may be challenging to turn her against you with how good and loyal she is, but I will succeed."

Ella went with the prince as he coaxed a confused Cinder from her chamber. She listened silently as he fed her lies of Ella's involvement in having her imprisoned.

Cinder was crying. "You must be mistaken. I spoke to Ella, but that is all. Why are you doing this?"

Prince Monticello was not gentle about pulling Cinder to the castle dungeons, and Ella watched as her sister was thrown, quite literally, into a cell by the prison guard. Cinder looked so out of place; her pretty face did not belong behind the prison wall.

Tanner clenched the bars. "What happened, Ella? What was in the prince's tower? Are you all right?"

Cinder got up on her knees and held onto the bars. "Ella, is that you?"

Ella took off her helmet and some of the heavier pieces of armor. She was glad that Tanner was in her presence as the look on Cinder's face frightened her, even when it was behind steel bars.

"What have you done, Ella?"

It was difficult for Ella to look at Cinder, knowing that she had stolen her keys and was responsible for Cinder's imprisonment, so she looked mostly at Tanner as she explained. "He keeps my father up there. Our father. There are others, but I don't know who. I don't know why." Ella knelt down in front of them and rested her head against the bars. "I don't know anything."

"But that can't be, Ella. The prince would never do something like that."

Tanner looked quickly at Cinder. "Yes, he could. And I'm sure he has." Tanner explained a little about how the prince was not trusted even among his knights and close acquaintances, many of whom were also not worthy of trust. He knelt down to face Ella. "Ella, are you all right?"

Cinder began to pace. Would she believe it now that it came from a strange knight behind prison bars rather than from her sister? "Ella, you must go to the king," Cinder said.

"I can't go to the king. I don't even belong in the castle."

"No, Ella. He is very kind, the queen also. They will listen to you. They will know how to help our poor father."

Ella looked at her sister. "Are you sure?"

"Yes, Ella. I am sure." Cinder came back to the bars. "Do you still have all of the keys?"

Ella shrugged. “I know where they are. That is, if they have not been bothered.”

Cinder was more earnest now. “There is a key that will let you into the tower on the east side of the castle. That is where the king and queen reside.”

Ella stood up and Tanner followed suit. “Why did none of the keys open the prince’s tower?”

“Nobody has access to the prince’s tower, not even the cleaning servants or me.”

“That explains why it is so filthy. You should see him, Cinder. You wouldn’t even recognize him. You don’t by chance have a key to get you and Tanner out, do you?”

Cinder bowed her head, as if it was all finally sinking in. “The prince keeps all of the prison and dungeon keys himself.” She looked at her sister again. “All of our fates rest with you now, Ella. Speak to the king. Try to help our dear father.”

Ella hugged her sister through the prison bars. Then she turned toward Tanner. “I know there is not much that you can do for her, but please watch after her.”

“I will, Ella. I promise. Put your armor back on so that the guards do not question you. Be careful.”

Ella covered herself once more with the armor she had placed on the floor while she visited with her prisoners, and then she climbed the seemingly endless staircase back up to the main castle floor.

Ella made her way back to the prince's tower for the basket of keys. She regretfully peeked in on her father before leaving.

The sun was beginning to rise and there was busyness in the halls as she made her way to the east tower. Men dressed in robes walked to and fro. The armor that was too big for her small frame clanged loudly as she walked, but it fit in among the clanking of other suits of armor walking about.

Ella spotted the prince and halted for a moment, afraid that he would notice her. She resumed when she found he was occupied in threatening two familiar men. Their names were Flesher and William, and they had just returned from an unsuccessful journey. At least, that was what Ella gathered as she walked past the scene.

The king and queen's tower door was grand. It was made of oak and had a design fashioned of steel. The crest of the king was carved into the center of the door. Ella easily found the key she was looking for, now that it was light. It was a different color from all the rest and also bore the crest of the king. Ella hesitated for a moment, not fully trusting her sister's promises that the king and queen were kind. Cinder had also believed that the prince was good.

Ella had to work up the courage to put the key in the lock. She thought of her father, then with conviction, she turned the key and pushed on the heavy door.

18

"Hello?" It felt as though she was shouting with only quiet and stillness about her. Ella removed the heavy armor and set it near the door.

The entry room was more splendid than anything Ella had ever seen or could have imagined. Everything, from the lights to the dark wood furniture and marble floor looked fancy, bright, and as though it had never been touched before. A crystal chandelier glistened and dangled from the center of the room, and bright blue drapes adorned the only window, which let in enough light to carry Ella through many dark and gloomy days.

There was no answer to her calls. Ella stepped in and continued to look around her. Books covered the shelves that lined almost the entire room, except for a few doors and a staircase that led to an upper chamber.

Ella walked up the staircase, trying to convince herself that somebody wicked could not live in such a beautiful place. The upper room was larger than the one below. Windows covered the entire circle, and it was completely surrounded by an observation deck. A woman sat on a chair covered in gold fabric, and a man with flowing, white hair was out on the deck looking through a strange contraption that Ella had never seen before. He looked very bizarre to Ella, indeed, as he pressed his eye to a long pole with a circle at each end, one of which was larger than the other. She waited, hoping they would notice her. After a great pause, she opened her mouth.

"I beg your pardon, your majesty. I was hoping that I could have a conversation with the king."

"Oh, hello there. My, you look so much like Cinder, one of the castle servants. Are you her sister?"

Ella took a few brave steps forward after hearing the gentle voice of the queen. "Yes, your majesty."

The queen called for the king. "Come in here, dear. Come and see how much this girl looks like our dear Cinder."

The king turned and squinted to see through the window. He entered through a glass door and smiled at Ella.

"Hello there, Ella. You do look a lot like your sister Cinder. Except you have beautiful honey-colored hair and hazel eyes, and I think you are a few inches taller than she."

The elegant king walked closer to Ella.

"Yes, I think you are a little taller." His eyes narrowed in on her, and he spoke softly, as if he had a secret. "And you are also brave. I am glad that you have come."

Ella hesitated, swallowed, then focused on her purpose for coming. "Good King, I am grateful for your words. I was afraid you might have me thrown in the dungeons. But now that I am here, I was hoping we could have a conversation."

"Of course, my child. What is it?"

"Well, Good King, it is my father." Ella looked into the eyes of the king and wondered what he knew already and what he did not. "The prince keeps him in the tower above his chamber. He is bound. And Cinder, my sister, and also one of your good knights, he has locked in prison. Please, sir, will you please help us?"

The king's eyes changed slightly. They were not as bright as when Ella had first greeted him. And his expression was more solemn. "Yes, yes, I watched your father come to the castle. I also saw Tanner return after leaving you at your home. And when Cinder did not come in this morning, I suspected that she too was in prison."

The greatness of the king was enough to keep Ella humble, so she continued her questions in a dignified manner. "Why have you not done anything for them? Surely you have power over the prince. You are the king."

"The prince has certain powers and allowances. That is something I cannot help. Sometimes I interfere, and sometimes I trust in those who are being affected to find their way out of his grasp. As for your father, it was his choice to listen to the prince. He came here to the castle of his own will. Even still, he could leave the tower if he chose."

"No, he could not! You should see him! The prince has completely taken over his mind!" Ella did not think that it might be a bad idea to yell at the king until she was already done. She retracted and was surprised that the king responded in kindness, with the same even tone he had spoken in before.

"No, there is still spirit in him yet. Your father's tree was one of the strongest in the kingdom. A tree like that is not easily taken. But, now that he has come this far, it will take a lot of time and effort for him to get roots again."

"But his tree has actually been chopped down. What then?"

"Chopping down a tree cannot kill its spirit. It may still grow yet again. And while the person connected to that tree may be injured in some way, they will most likely survive." The king looked at Ella with his clear, blue eyes. "There is something else that you must understand: because your father has allowed the prince to lead him into darkness, he currently does not have a strong connection with his tree. It hangs by a thread. But a single thread is still a connection. There remains hope, Ella."

None of this made any sense to Ella, but suddenly she had a new purpose. "Does the prince have a tree?" Ella asked with a child's feigned innocence and curiosity.

"Yes, a dark and twisted tree." He spoke slowly and as if with a mix of anger and sadness.

"I have already taken up much of your time, Good King. I will leave you now."

Ella was about to turn when the king unexpectedly reached his arms forward and wrapped them around her. It was a truly affectionate hug, filled with real love, strength, and concern. It had been a long time since Ella had been held that way.

"I am glad you came, Ella. You are welcome anytime. And whatever you do, be careful. I will be watching out for you. I can see the entire kingdom from my tower windows." He smiled at her.

"Thank you," Ella said.

The queen smiled at Ella and embraced her as well. "Try not to worry about Cinder and Tanner. I am sure they will be all right."

Ella took her words to heart, and in that moment, she knew what she had to do. After leaving the tower of the king and queen, Ella put on her borrowed armor again. She walked down the castle corridors and shoved away every noise and distraction. She had to find the prince's tree. And there was no time to waste, not even for good-byes.

19

If a horse could look uncertain, that is certainly how Cassandra looked as Ella pulled her with no small effort from the stable outside the kingdom castle. The horse took a step forward and then stalled. Ella pulled again. Cassandra took another step and waited. Ella pulled with all her might again. A few more steps were all Ella could get out of her. Cassandra even bent down to try and pick up a few forgotten oats. Ella pulled once more, letting out a loud, angry grunt, and the horse finally obeyed.

Ella may have ridden almost comfortably, with her borrowed armor resting on the side of the horse instead of on her person, except she had no experience with steering. It took longer than it would have for a skilled rider, but Ella eventually reached her childhood home. She entered with the hope of going unnoticed. At first, she was. Katrina was behind a locked door, which Beatrice was pounding against from the outside with both fists. Their mother was doing her usual activity.

The first thing Ella did was change out of her father's clothing. A dress would not fit well under armor, but she had felt awkward in pants and a shirt—especially when she had visited with the king and queen—and wanted the comfort of her favorite dress.

There was a single bookshelf standing in the upper hallway of the cottage. Using a lit candle, Ella sorted through all of the books, hoping to find a map. At this she was unsuccessful. Her search continued under each bed and each piece of furniture in disarray, and in every drawer. When that also proved fruitless, she slowly approached her mother.

"Mother, it is Ella. I was wondering if we had any maps of the kingdom in the house."

"I'm sorry, child, I'm too busy right now to help you."

Ella was happy that her mother at least seemed to be recognizing her, even if she wasn't being helpful, until her mother spoke again.

"Perhaps one of my daughters could help you."

Ella's heart sank. Each time she walked toward her mother it was with hope, even if that hope was small, and every time she walked away, it was with a sad heart and disappointed spirit. She turned to leave once more. It didn't matter to her that it was getting late. Ella would have preferred to sleep in the snow than under the roof she was currently standing beneath.

"What are you doing here?" Katrina asked as she came down the stairs. "I thought you moved away or something. Isn't there somewhere else that you could go?"

Ella briefly thought of telling Katrina about father. She laughed out loud when the thought crossed her mind to ask for her help.

"What's so funny?"

Ella thought of several answers—your hair, your face, your ridiculous dress—none of which she shared out loud. She also thought of what Katrina would say if she did ask her for help. Most likely it would be something like, "Father? I don't give a snit about father unless you think he will come home rich enough to buy me my own castle and giant-sized closet full of dresses and shoes."

Katrina grew impatient with Ella's silence. "Mother, how do I look tonight?" Katrina's evil smile told Ella that she knew their mother paid no attention to her third daughter and that Katrina enjoyed rubbing it in.

Their mother turned her head to see. "You do look lovely. Have a wonderful time, dear."

"Where are you going this time of night?" Ella asked.

"I'm going out."

"You can't go out so late. And especially not dressed like that. You look like a . . . You may very well be mistaken for a . . . Where are you going this time of night?"

"How dare you? Just because I actually have a man who loves me and thinks I'm beautiful. You are no longer my sister."

Ella wondered if she would ever meet this boy from the village that took girls out of their house at strange hours. She wondered if their mother had taken the time to meet him.

Katrina took an excessive amount of time stomping around the house gathering her things and then huffed out the door.

Ella peeked out the window to get a look at the boy. It was someone she had seen once or twice in the village, the shoemaker's son. They were ridiculous with their giggling and batting eyes. Ella watched them get into the horse-drawn cart and ride out of sight.

With the house quiet again, Ella could hear Beatrice's whimpers. A newfound compassion filled Ella's heart. Maybe it was because the cries actually sounded sincere and were not loud enough to cause any deafness. Ella walked up the stairs to find her sister sitting against a wall. She knelt beside her and put her arms around her. "Come here, little one."

Beatrice wasn't really little anymore. Ella couldn't believe how much she had grown in the three months that she had been away and in the last few years that Ella really hadn't paid any attention to her. She was eleven years old now but still acted very much like a young child.

"You have to go to bed now. But do you know what?" Ella was being mysterious.

"What?"

"I am going on a quest. Just like one of the king's knights. I have a horse and a sword and everything."

"You do not."

"Yes, I do." Ella hugged her sister lightly before standing up. "Come here. I will get you to bed."

Ella helped Beatrice off of the floor and to their room. It was pitch black in the cottage now except for the light their mother worked by and the candle Ella carried. Ella set the candle on the table beside the bed, felt around for the blanket, and placed it over her sister.

Should she tell her? "I am going to try to help Father," Ella said before thinking it through.

"Father?" Beatrice perked up instantly.

"Yes. I am going to try." Ella stroked her sister's hair for a moment. "I'm sorry that I have been so mean to you for all of these years, Beatrice. I hope you can forgive me."

"I love you, Ella." A person always loves to be called by their name, and those were three words that Ella had not heard for a long time. She wiped a few tears from her face and kissed her sister on the head.

"Good-bye now, Beatrice."

"Good-bye." Beatrice closed her eyes, and Ella descended to the main floor of the cottage.

Ella watched the delicate motions of her mother's arms as she fed the wool into the wooden spinner. "Good-bye, Mother," she said before turning around and walking out the door.

20

Ella walked outside to find that Cassandra had abandoned the quest. Ella debated for a long time after that about what to do next. She sat down on the steps and considered the possibility of rescuing Cinder and Tanner from prison; it seemed impossible. She thought of her geography lessons and wondered how long it would take to walk the entire kingdom. Searching for Cassandra would surely be pointless. She would have to go alone. But where?

There had been a place on the Robinson's map that Ella remembered was shaded in gray. She wanted to begin looking for the prince's tree there. She knew it was far away from Willow Top, but that was about all she could remember. It was even farther away from the kingdom castle. And it wasn't anywhere near Shepherd's Glade or Riverwood. The shaded area was at the southern tip of the kingdom. Ella closed her eyes and pictured the map. There was a village called Twin Pines. It was marked on the map by two identical pine trees. Behind it was a thick pine forest, and behind the pine forest was the shaded area. It was not marked on the map by any symbol or name.

Ella looked toward the castle, remembering the king's words. The thought of him and the beauty within that part of the castle gave her strength. She hesitated as she placed her right foot onto the dirt road in front of her mother's house, but then, with certitude, she walked blindly into the night.

Ella generally had a good sense of direction. But without a map, a compass, or any experience in the area that she was wandering through, Ella easily lost her way. The only familiar sight was the waning moon hanging in the sky almost directly over her head. The only familiar sound was the whispering of the aspen leaves in the gentle wind. With no hope of finding her way in the dark, and not wanting to get too far off the path, Ella decided to sleep until morning, when she would at least be able to see the earth on which she walked.

Sleep was not easy to find. With all of the worry and responsibility now on her shoulders, and with her fear of the darkness and unknown, Ella was much more comfortable with her eyes open. But it didn't matter whether her eyes were open or closed. Either way her imagination would invent a shadow or some face or figure. She was even sure that she heard rustling on the ground not far from where she was resting.

That was when she tightly closed her eyes and waited. She painted a picture in her mind of the scene in front of her—tall, slender shadows of trees, an occasional body of bush, and empty blackness. She did not open her eyes again until she was convinced that those were the only things in front of her. The ground was colder than it had been while sleeping outside on the way to the castle from Riverwood. Thoughts of the kind family there and of the knight, with his goodness—not to mention his clumsiness—were enough of a distraction for Ella to relax a little.

It grew increasingly colder throughout the night, and while it wasn't quite light enough to discern which way she would go, Ella could at least see each shape and figure for what it really was.

Ella rose and began walking simply to bring the temperature of her body back up. It wasn't long before the sun began brightening the tips of the aspen trees. Ella could now see the path that led back to her home. She had not gotten off of it by far, but it was barely wide enough to fit a coach and easily mistaken for some other clearing between all of the trees. She knew that she had to pass through a town called Cobblestone, which she had never been to before, and that she would reach the town around nightfall.

She walked quickly the whole day and spent her time thinking of things that she might say to persuade someone to give her a warm place to sleep for the night.

Prince Monticello woke early that morning to find a servant taking his latrine.

"What are you doing in here?" he asked her.

"I am cleaning your chamber, sire," the girl said as she bowed to the floor.

"Nobody is allowed into my chamber until after eleven o'clock! Didn't Cinder tell you that?"

"Cinder is nowhere to be found, sir. There are rumors that she may be in prison."

The prince lay back down on his bed and stared at the ceiling. There wasn't a servant in the entire kingdom that could run the castle as smoothly as Cinder had. But what was he to do after having Cinder thrown in prison? He sent the girl away and began spinning a new web.

Cinder and Tanner had no expectations of seeing the prince but anxiously awaited Ella and the news she would bring. They both rushed to the bars of their individual cells when they heard footsteps on the way to the lower prison dungeons. The flowing robes of the prince were not a pleasant sight to either one of them.

Monticello walked straight to Cinder, followed by a prison guard. "I am having you released for questioning, Cinder of Willow Top. Please follow me."

The guard unlocked the cell. Cinder queried the prince with her eyes.

Tanner went unnoticed by them all. He and Cinder had not conversed much since Ella had left. Tanner was too shy, too worried about his fellow prisoner's sister, and too hungry and tired to speak.

Cinder did not know the full story of Ella and Tanner, or she may have shown more interest in the knight.

Cinder reluctantly but obediently followed the prince and guard. The guard stopped at the upper level, but Cinder continued to follow Monticello to his private chambers.

They entered the room, and the prince closed the door behind them and then turned to face Cinder. "It is regrettable that I had to put you in prison, but I hope that you will be able to help me sort out some things. Your sister has been quite a bit of trouble to me lately, as you well know."

That wasn't true. Cinder didn't really know what was going on. "What do you mean, your majesty?"

The prince sat down at his desk, which was covered with half-written letters as well as fresh parchment, an ink well, and several quills. He shifted the objects on his desk as he spoke. "I had you put in the prison dungeon because your sister convinced me that you helped her try to kill me."

Cinder squinted at the prince. "What are you talking about?"

Monticello looked into her eyes. "Do you know where your sister is?"

"No, your majesty. She was supposed to come and find us after she spoke to the king. She told me about our father and how you keep him prisoner above this very room." Cinder had never been able to produce a mean or forceful voice well. Apparently, there wasn't time to change that now.

"Come with me." The prince stood from his dark chair and led the way.

Cinder followed the prince out of his chamber and up to the tower above. It was modestly decorated in purple and scarlet, but there was not a soul present in the room.

"As you see, I keep nothing in my upper chamber but a rather small library. It would seem that I am not the only one your sister lies to." The prince watched Cinder carefully. Would she believe him this time? She had to.

His glare penetrated through her, even though she was not looking at him. Instead her eyes were shifting about the room, trying to focus on something and find some clarity.

All of the books were too far away to read their titles, and the curtains were mostly drawn so that not much light was coming through the windows.

"She is missing now," the prince began. "Not one person in this castle knows where she has gone." The prince chose his next words carefully. "I know that you are innocent, Cinder. And everyone in the castle, even the castle itself, groans because you and your efforts have been greatly missed, even in this one morning of your absence."

Cinder pondered all of his words before responding. "What is it that my sister is accused of?"

"She tried to kill me." The prince pulled out a knife from his cloak. "Do you recognize this?"

Cinder closed her anguished eyes. "Yes. That is a knife from my family kitchen. They were passed to my mother from my father's mother. They bear the family seal."

"Correct. You see, your sister tried repeatedly to thrust this knife into my heart. Lucky for me, she is a great deal smaller and weaker than myself, and has very poor aim." The prince walked closer to Cinder to show how tall he was. "She also makes a poor knight." It was only in that last sentence that he began to lose his coolness and allow his anger to seep through his gritted teeth as he spoke. He was able to collect himself again, however, almost immediately.

Cinder looked around the room, trying to feel any remnants of her father's spirit, if he had, in fact, been there as Ella had said. She felt nothing. The room looked and smelled precisely as the room below them. She did not want to believe the prince, but his evidence was irrefutable.

"I, along with all of my aides and advisors, would like to reinstate you as mistress of managing affairs. However, I need a couple of things from you first." He knew he had won her again.

"How can I be of help, your majesty?" Cinder bowed her head and clasped her hands in front of her.

"Your sister used your position, not to mention your keys, to locate me in the castle. The fact that she had your basket of keys was the reason why you were placed in the prison dungeon in the first place. I need a statement of your innocence."

Cinder looked straight into his cool, blue-gray eyes. "I truly can attest to that, sir. Ella came to me but left empty-handed." Cinder bowed her head again. "We actually quarreled a bit." Cinder played with her hands, ashamed for having failed Ella, and then looked back at the prince. "She must have returned to my room and stolen the keys. They were still in their rightful place when I went to sleep."

"That will be good enough." Prince Monticello stepped closer to her and spoke softly. "One more thing, and you can resume your duties."

Cinder waited for his instructions.

"I need you to go and search your family home. If she is not there, you may return alone. If she is there, all I need is for you to bring her back to the kingdom castle. Either way, you will have your position again. I need you here to organize the servants, and my aides are simply lost without you. As am I."

Monticello reached out for Cinder's face and moved the back of his fingers across her cheek. He spoke in hushed, affectionate tones. "I am sorry for having you imprisoned too hastily. I should have known you would never be involved in such things. I have missed seeing your beautiful face and ashen hair. And, if it is not too late to win your trust, I would still like to have you as my guest at the next ball. It is scheduled for the end of this very week."

Cinder was torn. It was one thing to go about her life at the castle. It was another to help the prince find her sister and have her punished, even if her crimes were serious. Cinder had a hard time believing it at first, but then she thought of her mother and other sisters and of how much they had changed. Nothing seemed impossible anymore. His eyes were so inviting, and his words so flattering, that Cinder could not resist. "I will do what you require."

"I am glad to hear it. Two of my finest aides will be escorting you."

Prince Monticello led Cinder down from the tower where two men were waiting for them, and it was now Cinder's turn to go on a journey with Flesher and William.

21

The road home was much shorter for Cinder than it had been for Ella. The horses were eager, and the coach driver was determined. Flesher and William must have been sworn to silence; Cinder did not hear them speak for the entire journey. She came to hate the way William looked at her, as if he had some secret joke and wouldn't share it. Occasionally she would watch Flesher's serious scowl as he peered outside the window.

"Mother?" Cinder called as she walked into the family home with the prince's two aides standing behind her.

"Oh, Cinderella, thank heavens you're here. Beatrice has not been outside for days and . . ."

"I can't stay, Mother. I came to see if Ella is here."

"Who?" The mother turned around for the first time.

"Ella, Mother. Have you seen Ella?" Cinder was not in the mood for playing games or repeating sentences.

"I do not know who you are talking about." She returned to her spinning and began to cry. "Cinderella, I am disappointed in you. You spend too much time away from home when you are needed here."

Flesher and William were surprised at the conversation.

"We'll have to search, miss," Flesher said, looking for the first time into Cinder's dark brown eyes.

Cinder showed the men upstairs. Katrina was still in bed and horrified when she saw two castle men come into her room before she was dressed and had combed her hair. They searched every room and cupboard as well as the grounds and part of the mountain.

"Well, the prince gave us until tomorrow to return with the girl if we found her." William said. "I hate to waste all the time that he so freely granted us. I say we go on an adventure."

"Please, sir. I would just like to get back to the castle." Cinder was relieved that they had not found Ella but wanted the comfort and familiarity of her work all the same.

Flesher was left to side with someone. "What did you have in mind, William?" he asked after briefly looking at Cinder. Truth be told, he was not anxious to be done spending time with her.

"Well, they make very fine wine in Cobblestone," William said.

"Cobblestone?" Cinder asked, her head tilting up toward him in interest.

"Yes," William said as he took two steps closer to her, "but more importantly, wine."

"All right. I do enjoy going to Cobblestone. They have the most beautiful shops."

"It's settled, then," Flesher added.

The three unlikely travel companions got into the coach once again and began their journey away from the castle. This time, they went down and across the mountain toward Cobblestone.

Ella's swift steps brought her to Cobblestone as the sun was just beginning to dim. She was grateful to have enough light to walk around the town and look for a place to stay. The only thing she had eaten all day was a bunch of red berries she had found in the forest, but she did not feel any hunger. Her legs ached, however, and she was thirsty.

Luck was definitely something that Ella had forgotten to bring with her. Each door that slammed in her face made this more apparent. One fat man whined about all of the beggars around. Another man told her that she was welcome to stay in exchange for serving food, washing dishes, and scrubbing all of the floors. Ella was much too tired for all of that and would rather sleep outside. The last place she tried was a cottage that reminded her so much of the Robinson's home that she couldn't resist simply knocking on the door to see who would open it. A gentle-looking woman answered the door. She wore an apron and was holding a child on her hip.

"Pardon me, ma'am. I am far away from home and was hoping to find a place to stay for the evening. Do you have a spare corner of your home I could borrow for the night?"

The woman glanced up for a moment as a coach from the kingdom castle drove by.

Cinder was not unaware of her sister standing on the porch of the house she passed. She nervously glanced at William and Flesher to see if they were looking out that way. William was whistling merrily but watching her with suspicious eyes, and Flesher was looking out the opposite side of the coach. Cinder paid attention to directions after that so she could find her way back to the house.

When the three companions reached the main square, they each went their separate ways, agreeing to be back within two hours so they could still get back to the castle in time to spend part of the night in their own beds. Cinder quickly walked back the way that they had come into town. She found the house easily. It was large and had many trees surrounding it. Glowing lights brightened almost every window.

"Hello, ma'am," Cinder said to the woman who answered the door. "I am looking for a girl who I saw speaking to you on this very porch only a few moments ago. Is she still here, or do you know where she has gone?"

Ella heard her sister's voice and excitedly came to the door. "Cinder? Cinder, is that you?"

Ella threw her arms around her sister in proclamation of her glee. But Cinder was stiff. "What is it, Cinder? Are you not happy to see me?"

Cinder beheld all of the people watching them. The woman stared, and three of her children followed suit.

Cinder whispered, "I need to speak to you, Ella."

Ella shivered as she heard Cinder's soft, cold voice. The two girls went outside after Ella begged the family to excuse her.

Ella wondered what had happened in the short time since she'd left. "Is it father?"

"No. It's you, Ella." Cinder stood with her arms folded, and her voice reflected a bit of cruelty. She had never spoken to Ella in such a tone.

"What about me?" It was always Ella. Everything was always her fault.

"The prince sent an expedition for you. We were to bring you back to the castle."

"I can't go back to the castle. How did you find me?"

"We only happened upon you. Actually, I have not revealed to my companions that I know where you are. I only saw you at this house as we passed by."

"What does the prince want with me?" Ella's voice showed signs of complete acceptance. For a moment, she couldn't believe that she had actually thought herself capable of destroying the prince or helping her family.

Cinder deepened her whisper. "You are wanted for trying to kill him." Cinder waited for a reaction, and a reaction she got.

"Yes, I tried to kill the prince! You would have too, Cinder—even you—if you had seen him as I did—our father."

"The prince showed me the room, Ella. There was nothing there. Nothing like what you described."

Ella held a hand to her head and caressed her own brow. Her hair fell forward and covered her face. She spoke softly, knowing it was hopeless. "He has deceived you, dear one."

"He had proof! You have none!"

"We are sisters!" Ella shot her eyes directly at Cinder's.

"I could be ruined, you know. The prince offered to give me my station back if I brought you to the kingdom castle. Will you ruin this chance for me?"

It wasn't like Cinder to be manipulative, and Ella worried that her sister might be falling under the prince's spells as their father had—all the more reason for Ella to continue on her quest. "Yes. I will resist every attempt you make to get me to return to the castle tonight."

"I have companions with me. Two of the prince's aides escorted me here. They could arrest you."

Ella folded her arms and leaned back slightly. "Well, go and get them then."

Cinder's gray hair began to look black in the ever-darkening night. She turned to leave.

"Can I give you some advice?" Ella called after her sister.

Cinder turned around to face the sister that she was considering betraying.

"I would stay closer to Flesher. William can be very ungentlemanly."

Cinder stared at Ella. How did she know who her travel companions were? She watched her for a moment longer and then walked into the darkness.

Ella took several deep breaths as she tried to decide what to do. She hoped that her sister really wouldn't bring William and Flesher to have her arrested, but she did not know whether she should fear it or not. The sweet woman who had offered her a place to sleep looked confused and suspicious as Ella told her that her sister had come for her and that she would no longer need a place to stay. As the door shut out the only light she would see that night, Ella ran into the woods.

Cinder and Flesher waited long for William. Drunken, he stumbled back to the square early in the morning. The three stepped into the coach once more for the ride back to the kingdom castle.

"Is everything all right, miss?" Flesher asked Cinder as William snored loudly.

Cinder quickly turned to him. "Yes, I'm all right. Just tired."

"I am sorry that we didn't find Ella. You must be worried about her."

"How do you know my sister?"

"William and I were to bring her back to the castle before. The knight we traveled with led her away from us, and we lost them. She is a kind girl."

Cinder listened to his words but did not know what to make of them. He sounded completely ignorant of what the prince had told her and of Ella's attempt to kill him. Flesher again interrupted her thoughts.

"Has your hair always been that color?" He pulled lightly at a few silver strands.

"Yes," Cinder said. "Ever since I was born. That is why my parents named me Cinder."

"It's beautiful." He mostly kept his eyes on her hair but managed to look into her eyes before losing his nerve.

"Thank you." It wasn't a compliment she received often, although people did ask her about it on occasion. Mostly they just stared, but if someone was brave enough to ask, "beautiful" was not usually the word they used to describe it, but rather "different," "interesting," or "amazing."

Cinder and Flesher exchanged one last look before he moved to look out the window.

When William woke up, he began trying to get Cinder to sit close to him. Cinder remembered her sister's words and remained close to Flesher. She even hooked her arm with his at one point, which made him squirm a bit, but at least it helped her feel safe. It wasn't difficult for Flesher to keep William in line, considering how absent the drunkard's mind was. In fact, a slight shove was all that was needed to knock him unconscious once again.

When they finally reached the castle, Cinder was relieved to be out of William's presence and wouldn't have minded if she never saw him again. Flesher had been a strange relief, but Cinder did not think of him again once she had stepped down from the coach.

Cinder sent word to the prince of what she had discovered, or rather, what she had not discovered. She kept it a secret—from everyone—that she had seen Ella in Cobblestone.

While she had considered telling William and Flesher when they were still in the village, it just wouldn't satisfy her. It hadn't helped that William was nowhere to be found. But, truth be told, Cinder was not ready to believe that her sister was a mad killer or that her prince was a devious fraud.

22

What did the prince want with Ella? Perhaps he saw her as a threat and had for a long time.

Ella did not realize this, but she had left an impression on the prince years ago. The prince had long been in the practice of evil—stealing lives through murder, stealing the virtue of women, stealing riches and possessions, stealing souls. All of these things were done by proxy, of course. It was his sick delight to see someone else hurt another, bringing about ruin to both the doer and the receiver.

The prince had begun a political campaign of sorts, as it was his desire to overthrow the king. He went door to door throughout the whole kingdom, accompanied by a party of men that he referred to as "soul catchers." They had been chosen carefully, and not a single one ever questioned him. In fact, out of fear, not one person in the entire kingdom questioned his motives or deeds in all those months. Not one, except for a small girl about the age of nine.

It was late. It was dark. And Prince Monticello and his men were making their last stop for the night at a cottage near Willow Top. Ella's mother and father had been discussing things like money and children and such while their daughters prepared for bed upstairs. A knock sounded at the door. The knocking alone—slow and intense—was enough to cause an eerie feeling to surface in Ella's gut. Adela answered the door. And even though her parents thought she was in bed, Ella was listening. She watched from the top of the stairs, dressed in a white nightgown, her hair still awaiting its nightly brushing and braid.

Prince Monticello looked normal enough, even if his clothes were finer than anything she had ever seen. His robe was long and trimmed with gold rope.

Ella thought it was strange that her parents were so cordial to the prince because he made her anxious. Ella glared at him from above. She did not understand much of anything that was said, except that he was the prince, the king was corrupt and leading the kingdom into a gulf (she wondered what a gulf was), and that the prince was looking for followers. Her father, much to her dismay, said that he would think it over. At one point, the prince turned to look at Ella, and she stuck out her tongue at him.

When Prince Monticello began to say his good-byes to her father and mother, Ella ran to her window to watch him mount his horse. Her sisters were already asleep. Prince Monticello looked up at her, and she glowered back with enough defiance and rebellion to cause him to flinch and fidget until even his horse became uneasy.

While Ella soon forgot all of this, especially when her father began to slip away, the prince would never forget her expression that night, as if she would hunt him down someday.

When Tanner brought Ella to the prince's attention, Monticello thought it only right to torture her a little. But things had gotten out of hand.

Prince Monticello sat in front of his fireplace as he read Cinder's letter about not having found Ella. His eyes blazed into the flames. He felt within him that Cinder's words were lies. He thought of how determined Ella had been to kill him. She would not give up. Perhaps it was time for the prince to pay a visit to his tree.

He would deal with Cinder later. It would do more damage to court her for a while before crushing her. The prince left his chambers to find one of his aides. There were horses to ready, things to gather, and an expedition to plan.

If the moon was in the sky that night, the clouds kept its whereabouts clandestine. Ella rested underneath a tree. She curled up as close to the trunk as she could get, even though she knew it would not keep her any warmer. Tears drew lines down her dirty face as she thought about how every time she met a member of her family, it seemed that they were there to discourage her, thwart her, or throw a stumbling stone right in front of her.

Her thoughts turned to the prince. She wondered at his darkness and what he was capable of. All of the difficulties her family was facing came back to the prince. If she could just get at him somehow, maybe everything would be different. But why had the king allowed all of this to happen in the first place?

Ella's discouragement turned to determination and her despair to eagerness before the break of morning. There is so much hope in a sunrise. Ella could see it peeking through a gap in the trees. She took in a deep, cool breath and began walking in the direction that she believed would lead her to Twin Pines.

The wood, which had been pleasant in the early morning, grew increasingly dark throughout the day. What began as tall, spread-out aspen and oak trees became a mess of thick, thorny bushes.

Blood trickled down one of Ella's arms after a thorn pricked it. She placed a hand over the spot to help the bleeding stop, but, eventually, she had too many cuts to cover with her hands. Most of the bushes came to just above her shoulders, although once in a while, they would brood down over her from far above. Each bush was an entanglement of branches and shoots that seemed to tie into knots with the bushes that surrounded it. It became thicker with each step, and Ella had to change directions often just to be able to walk. She kept trying to change back to her original direction, but the brush was simply too thick. She might have suffocated if she had insisted on going in the direction she believed would lead her to the gray area she remembered from the map.

The day wore on in darkness. Ella was hungry but not tired. The thought of lying down among the thorns and pokes was enough to keep her awake and alert. At last, the shrubbery began to thin again. In the distance, Ella could see the eerie shadows of a pine forest. She switched courses once again and headed for the village of Twin Pines.

23

A knight who is falsely imprisoned and forced to worry about the girl he loves may well go mad. He will at least act out of desperation at times.

The guard employed in the prison dungeons escorted a castle servant down to exchange the latrine as he did once every day. Tanner was unarmed. The guard wasn't. But the guard found it difficult to fight back when he had a smelly, waste-filled bucket stuck on his head. The servant, an elderly man with long, white hair, looked shocked but did not pursue Tanner. He did, however, yell a warning before stooping down to help the filthy knight.

The prince would usually only spare one knight at a time to guard the prison dungeons. But it became obvious to Tanner as he was stopped on the upper level by a knight in full armor with drawn sword, that two guards were necessary while the latrines were exchanged. Since he no longer had a bucket, Tanner resorted to begging. The guard was not a stranger to him; Tanner knew all of the knights in the castle.

"Why should I help you?" the other knight asked.

"Because I am an innocent man sitting in prison while an evil prince walks free and a fair maiden is surely in danger."

The guard knew he spoke the truth. Most of the knights were convinced of the prince's evil.

"What about my head? The prince will never believe that you bested me in a fight when I am armed and you are not."

"Maybe you need to stop thinking about your head and remember that you also have a heart."

The knight begrudgingly let Tanner slip from the room. He regretted it once he saw the mess that had been left downstairs.

Tanner first found his way to the armory to steal armor and weapons. That proved much easier than escaping prison. He then made his way to the kingdom castle stables to find that Cassandra was not tied up as she had been when they arrived at the castle. A quick search around the stables led to her whereabouts. She was grazing on some long grass that grew just outside the castle wall.

"Come here, girl," Tanner coaxed as he held out a handful of oats from the stable.

Cassandra looked at him momentarily and then resumed her meal.

"How did you get out here, girl?" Tanner spoke to her softly, trying to piece the puzzle together in his head. "Have you seen Ella? Did she ride you somewhere? Did you leave her alone or have you brought her back?"

A sword and full armor were still strapped to the horse. Tanner considered the possibilities. He could have passed Ella in the castle corridors unknowingly. "Where is she, girl?"

Cassandra whinnied as if to ask for privacy while she ate.

"She would have tied you up, wouldn't she? Cassandra, you must take me to her." Tanner climbed onto the strong horse, and she seemed bothered by his tugs and kicks as he settled himself into place. But as soon as he was firmly mounted, Cassandra rode fast all the way to the cottage in Willow Top.

"Is she really here, girl?" he asked the horse before she slowed enough for him to dismount.

Tanner slipped off the horse and tied her up much better than Ella had. He approached the cottage and knocked on the door. Nobody answered, but Tanner attributed that to the fact that such a roar was coming from inside. He was sure nobody could even hear his knocking. He beat the door louder, and when that didn't work, he kicked it repeatedly until Katrina finally answered. She looked very pleased to see a handsome knight at her door. Her head poked out, and she closed the door on her own neck as far as she could to hide the inner turmoil from his view.

"How can I help you?" Her smile was pretend, her eyes filled with attempted charm, and her hair a mess.

"I am looking for Ella. Is she here?"

"Sir, I'm afraid that no one by that name lives here."

"Is she your sister?"

Katrina's next words were spoken proudly. "I used to have a sister named Ella. But I don't anymore. Is there anything else that I can do for you?"

Tanner whispered a plea. "Please, miss. She could be in great danger. If you know anything about where she is or where she has been, I would be pleased to hear it."

The door closed hard onto Katrina's head as Beatrice let out a loud wail.

Katrina kicked Beatrice from behind, just like a horse, and then cried out, "Well, that would serve her right, wouldn't it? She does nothing around here!"

"I want Cinderella! I want Cinderella!" Beatrice yelled as she kept trying to close the door on her sister.

Tanner did not want to leave without searching the house. He was a bit afraid to enter, however.

"Who is Cinderella?" he asked as Katrina won the battle and made her way to the porch, managing to close the door behind her. She had to keep a strong grip on the door handle to keep Beatrice from coming out as well.

"Cinderella is our sister. She works at the castle. Perhaps you know her. If you do, I think you should tell her to come home right away and do her chores. Beatrice is completely out of control, Mother is beside herself, and I have a date tonight."

Tanner was done whispering. He was done being patient altogether.

"Miss! I'm afraid that this is a matter that comes directly from the castle and the prince himself. I will have to come inside and search the house. I will also need to question anyone else inside."

All at once, the color was erased from Katrina's face. She did not want to let the knight into her home, knowing what a horrible mess it was. "Fine. But don't blame me if the little brat rips your head off."

Katrina opened the door again and walked through. Tanner followed. The sight in front of his eyes was beyond anything he had ever seen before. A woman sat in a makeshift room at a spinning wheel. She did not turn to greet him. Beatrice scowled at Katrina. There was not a spot on the floor where the knight could place his foot without stepping on something; clothing, dishes, wooden toys, food, pillows, blankets, torn pieces of cloth, clumps of long hair, and mismatched shoes all littered the floor.

Tanner first approached the woman.

"Excuse me, ma'am. You must be the lady of the house."

The mother turned around to show her faint face. "Did you come from the castle? Is Cinderella here too?"

"No, ma'am. I have come looking for Ella." He spoke gravely as he studied the woman he knew must be Ella's mother.

"I do not know who you mean." Her eyes were empty and her voice thin, but somehow her hair had managed to stay long and beautiful over all the years.

Perhaps it was because Cinder took the time to brush it whenever she came home.

Tanner was not prepared for an answer like that. He looked around the room again, searching for any clue or indication that he was in the right place. There was nothing to remind him of Ella; even the mother and two sisters had dark hair and brown eyes, giving no signal that they could be relatives.

His gaze returned to the mother, who was anxious to get back to her spinning. "Surely you know who I mean. I left Ella here only a few days ago. Did you not see her at all?"

"Oh," Adela said. "I do remember seeing another girl here besides my two daughters. I'm not entirely sure what she was here for."

"Is she not also your daughter, ma'am?"

"I have three daughters: Katrina, who you see standing by the door, Cinderella, who works at the castle, and Beatrice, who has made a mess of this house and who will not stop bothering me." She whipped around and began spinning again.

Ella had been right when she had said that it would only take two minutes for him to understand what state her family was in and why she had been so hesitant to return home. But he couldn't fathom why the woman did not mention Ella as a daughter nor why Cinder carried Ella's name on the end. At this point, he thought it would be best if he bowed out without any further questions or even searching.

"Pardon me, ma'am. I must be at the wrong house." Tanner backed away from the spinner and tripped over a shoe. He fell onto his backside, which produced an arrogant chuckle from Katrina. After he was on his feet again, Tanner almost ran back to Cassandra in a hurry to escape the house and begin searching for Ella elsewhere.

"Wait!" a voice called after him. Beatrice stood on the porch with her arm up in the air. Under closer scrutiny, Tanner saw her worn, soiled dress that was too small for her. Her hair was tangled, and her face was dirty. "Ella was here," she said.

Tanner walked closer to the girl. "You've seen Ella?"

"Yes. Not long ago."

He placed a hand on the girl's shoulder and spoke with earnestness. "Did she say where she was headed?"

"Not really. Except that she was going to try to help our father."

Tanner watched the girl as he thought about what that might mean. He thought of their conversation about the legend of the trees, and it didn't take him long to decide to head south.

24

When Ella reached the border of the pine forest, at last something was familiar. Two pine trees stood tall above the ground. The trees may have been identical once, but one was mostly dead, with only a few green needle-filled limbs in the center of the tree and one toward the very top.

Ella entered through the center of the two pines. It was difficult to tell that there had once been inhabitants. Every sparse structure that she inspected was abandoned. At least she could spend the night under a roof without having to speak to anyone.

Even though she was alone, Ella felt completely surrounded. There was something about the pine forest that was infinitely more frightening than a grove of aspen trees. She rested on a dust-covered bed in the upstairs room of what must have been an inn. There were no blankets left, and Ella struggled not to shiver.

She needed sleep, but Ella could only taste fear, and wakefulness made her feel protected. The sounds of owls and coyotes added to her anxiety. They were foreign to a girl whose area of the woods produced sparrows and deer.

A rumbling sounded from a fireplace in the room, and Ella's heart changed tempo immediately. The noise became louder and louder until a cylinder of blackness escaped from the fireplace at great speed. Ella watched as a stream of seemingly angry bats flew straight out the window. None of them came close to her, but their screeching turned her skin cold and caused the hair on her body to point up.

The room turned black as the last glow of dusk retreated. Ella began thinking of all the places that she should be instead. Strangely, home was the first place that came to mind. She should have been at home, with a loving mother, father, and sisters. Second, if home was not a possibility, she should have been in Riverwood, where a second family and an occupation waited for her. Last, she thought of Tanner. Giving up her family and even her beloved home in Riverwood would have been easy if she could be with the good knight who had come for her. Now he was in prison, and it was possible that the prince had thrown Cinder back in prison as well. Ella wondered if Paul and Fern would have done anything to help her if she had gone to them. Did they love her enough? Did they love her at all?

All of these thoughts caused Ella's eyes to become heavy, and she fell asleep without realizing she had grown tired enough to forget her fears.

It only took a few hours for Tanner to reach the entangling thicket. He had pressed Cassandra for speed, giving her a swift kick in the gut whenever he felt she wasn't going fast enough. Rather than try to tackle the thicket in the darkness, he made a camp to rest for the night. Despite the cold air, he did not start a fire, knowing that the prince or a band of knights might be after him. Cassandra seemed nervous. She stepped lightly while tied to a tree and pulled on the rope occasionally as if she was trying to get away.

"Settle down, girl. Everything will be all right," Tanner assured her while he lay down on the hard ground.

The breeze rustling through the trees that night would have been comforting if it had not been so cold. Tanner shivered as he thought of Ella. He wanted to make sure he found her in time to get her far away from Twin Pines and what lay beyond.

All of the knights at the kingdom castle knew where the trees of the kingdom's royalty grew. Given what Beatrice had told him, Tanner guessed Ella must be after the prince's tree. He hoped he was right and that he would indeed find her traveling in this direction. And if he was right, he needed to reach her before the prince did.

Tanner forced himself to sleep; he needed all of his strength to press on in the morning, and speed was imperative.

Prince Monticello had no way of knowing for sure where Ella really was. He was acting on a feeling that had come based on how determined she had been to hurt him. Anyone who knew about the legend of the trees knew that you could harm a person by harming his or her tree. And even though the prince's tree did not need protection, if Ella was going to hunt it down, he was going to be there.

The prince rose early, but his escorts were already waiting for him.

"You'll need armor, men," he said sternly as he walked outside the castle where the horses and men were waiting.

The prince mounted his white horse while a few servants took the aides to the armory. Flesher and William were nowhere in sight. They were most likely avoiding the prince after having failed their last two missions. The three men that would ride with the prince knew him well. The prince's aides were the most loyal to him. Each was as skilled in defense and weaponry as any knight in the kingdom, and they were all looking for Ella.

"Where are we going, your grace?" one of the men asked. He was the largest of the three, with gruff facial hair and a determined, fear-provoking look on his face.

"We ride to Stoneland," the prince said so that only those closest to him could hear. The horse lifted up its front legs and let out a grumble that sounded more like it should have come from a bear. The prince's dark cape flew behind him as he and his men began their ride to the home of the prince's tree.

25

Ella did not sleep well. The bed felt more like a cliff rock with jagged edges and uneven slopes and angles. She watched the black night out of the uncovered window until the darkness turned into light by slight degrees. Once it was light enough to see that the images out of the window were trees and not prowling people or creatures, Ella got up and spent several minutes stretching her arms, back, and legs.

Outside the building, Ella had a difficult time determining which direction was which. The pine forest was so thick that she couldn't see anything else, not even the thicket or any mountains. Ella walked back to the entrance of Twin Pines in order to reorient herself a little.

She found her way back through the village easily after that, but it still felt as if the town had a presence, even in the dim light of morning.

Clouds thickened and brewed until it looked much like dusk or dawn. Then the clouds settled into place, not allowing any increase of sunlight and staying the same level of intolerable gray.

The village was small, with only a single street and a few outer-lying houses that she could see. Each window was either boarded or showed its broken glass. Spider webs were visible on several of the small buildings, one of them as large as the pony Ella's family had owned when she was a small child.

With each step, Ella moved farther away from the village and deeper into an ever-thickening wood. The air grew heavy until she had a feeling of being engulfed with fog, even though all of the clouds were far above her. It would not have surprised her to learn that she was being watched or followed, but she never saw anyone.

Ella studied the pines, each of which seemed to have its own distinctness. Some were tall and slender. There were new, young pines and old, crumbling pines. One of them looked as if it was bowing to her as she passed it. From some of them came creaking or cracking noises.

As she walked, small, twisted twigs became visible. They stemmed up from the ground, were black, and at first were no bigger than her hand. She continued on and found that with each step they increased in number and size. Eventually, it looked like a thicket of molasses-colored, bare bushes was trying to take over the pines. One such bush had even wound itself completely around a pine tree, and the pine's life was dwindling.

The pine forest thinned and the dark thicket grew and grew. Ella began to feel as she had the day before—that if she did not change directions she would soon begin to suffocate in the bushes. She also felt a little discouraged. Perhaps the black thicket was all that was there; a gray spot on a map couldn't have been more fitting for what she was walking through.

Then, suddenly, the thicket was gone, and an open space made a circle around a single tree.

Tanner was lost. It was frustrating to be a brave and honorable knight and have such a poor memory. Part of their training as knights had taken place in that very thicket. A maze had been created and the knights had been charged to find their way using the sun as their only source of direction. But the sun was no help now because of the thick clouds that covered it and most of its light. The maze was obviously grown over, as it had taken up most of the thicket, and Tanner had nothing to go on. Not to mention that he had left Cassandra tied up some time ago when she stubbornly refused to take another step into the thorny thicket.

A distant voice shouted, and Tanner recognized it as the prince's.

"We're almost there, men!"

Tanner heard the pounding of horses riding in the distance past where he stood. He ran after them, following their sound as long as he could until he was certain he was once again headed in the right direction. He was desperate for Cassandra now, knowing that the prince was headed toward Ella. But it would have been foolish to go back for her and lose his way again. Once he reached the twin pine trees that stood outside the thicket, he began to run as fast and as long as his legs would allow.

26

"You are so predictable, Ella." The prince's smooth voice was penetrating and caused Ella to shudder.

One of the prince's aides had enough bravery to question the prince. "What did we need armor for? She's as big as a mouse. And unarmed." He laughed, as did two of the other men.

The prince ignored them, and so did Ella. Monticello may have let it go because they were taunting Ella more than they were defying him.

"I am not afraid to die." Ella looked behind her to meet his eyes. She was kneeling down and had been trying to decide what to do with the tree now that she had found it. There was nothing to start a fire with, and every tool she had brought on her journey that may have helped had trotted off with Cassandra when the horse had left her. "Maybe it is you who should be afraid to die." Ella's voice was calm but threatening.

"Such harsh words when I have only come to bring you a gift."

Ella watched skeptically as the prince dismounted and unloaded a large sack from his horse. The horse seemed uneasy at the prince's every movement. Prince Monticello smiled as he walked toward Ella. "For you," he said as he held out the sack.

Ella did not want to take anything from the prince. She stared at the black cloth sack and tried to think of what dark magic might be inside.

"Well, aren't you ungrateful?" The prince dropped the sack in front of Ella. There was a dense thud, which filled Ella with a mixture of wonder and dread. Prince Monticello turned once more toward his horse. His men all looked puzzled but did not move or speak. Their faces were like stone as they watched the prince straddle the horse again.

"Oh, and by the way," the prince began before turning his horse around. "I have released your sister from prison. She has been pardoned. In fact, she will be escorting me to my next ball."

"Stay away from her," Ella commanded.

"To the castle, men!"

The four men all shouted orders to their horses. Ella waited for their exit to become embarrassing when the horses shied away from the thicket. But it was the thicket that became shy. As the prince and his men approached the dark, twisted mess of trees, the tangled twigs and branches bent and scooted to make a path for them. Ella could not believe her eyes. Even knowing that the prince had dark and magic ways, she had to wonder if what she had seen was real or an illusion. She knew the prince was capable of entrapping her in both and had a brief moment of hysteria, worrying that she was already caught in such a trap.

Her eyes eventually turned to the sack. Was it safe to open it? She carefully took a step toward it, and when nothing happened, she took another. When her feet were close to the sack, she bent down and placed her hand upon it. There were no sparks or spells or even any feelings of danger. Ella lifted the pack and shook it. It sounded as if it was full of metal. She untied the knot and, rather than taking a look inside, dumped the contents onto the ground. What she beheld was quite shocking. The prince had supplied her with everything she had been wishing she had brought with her—an ax, a shovel, and stones for making fire.

"What trickery have you brought here?" Ella whispered.

She placed the tools back in the sack and carried them to the tree. Then she examined the dark mass as she circled it. The king had been right. It was dark and twisted—the branches went in every direction—and it filled Ella with a bit of terror. But being in its presence was nothing like being in the same room as the prince. Since Tanner had chopped her father's tree, and it hadn't killed him, she decided to start with fire. Ella created sparks with the stones and lit a pile of kindling. Then she placed a small, dead tree branch in the flames until it was ablaze. She held the branch on the prince's tree until it nearly burned her fingers. The branch fell and burned until it became ash in front of her, but the tree was unaffected.

She tried digging next. The ground was solid. It was as hard, flaky, and impossible to dig into as fired clay. Ella slammed the point of the shovel into the ground repeatedly and at every possible place around the entire tree.

Ella rested for a moment, having exhausted herself trying to get a hole started with the shovel. The ax had a large wooden handle. The blade shone brightly, even without the light of the sun to cause a reflection. Ella reached for it but without hope that it would be able to do any damage to the black tree. She gripped the handle with both hands and rotated her arms back before swinging it with great force into the trunk. Her hands burned and tingled immediately. The shock had been so great that she didn't really know if the blow had done anything to the tree. She tried again, keeping her focus on the ax, watching it hit the tree. The same feeling came into her hands and up to her elbows, but nothing happened to the tree. Ella inspected the blade. It was slightly bent.

Ella fell to her knees. Night was approaching, and Ella knew she would not make it back out of the thicket before dark. Her hands became a bowl shape, and Ella placed her head inside. The bowl caught her tears and muffled her cries. She had never felt so alone and defeated as she did at that moment. Going back seemed pointless now. She looked toward the thicket and realized that every individual brush was a miniature copy of the prince's tree. Maybe the master tree could not burn, but perhaps those in the thicket could.

Ella grabbed the fire stones and walked over to the brink of the thicket. She knelt, on one knee this time, and smacked and rubbed one rock against another. Sparks flew the very first time and only increased as she smacked more intensely. The dry, dead pine needles on the ground caught fire easily, and the fire spread rapidly. So rapidly, that Ella found herself completely surrounded by fire before she could think to run to the other side of the circle. Panic swirled inside her head. Smoke engulfed the open space that was her only protection. Ella fell to the ground, and everything became dark.

27

When a room is dark, it only takes a tiny portion of sunlight to come in, and the room will be made light and visible again. A light came to Ella so that she could see everything that was happening. There was a tree—elevated in the air, glowing white and magnificent—that came down into the circle. It did not catch fire, and its brightness was not diminished by the smoke that filled the air. Ella stood up and began climbing the tree. Once she reached the first limb, she and the tree were lifted up, and Ella was carried away from the fire.

The fire spread, but not enough to cause worry for Twin Pines or any of the pine forest. After Ella had been set down on the ground again, it began to rain. She watched the glowing tree, which she now saw had dangling apples, as it moved through the sky and away from her until it vanished altogether.

In the pouring rain, the fire got smaller and smaller until it died out completely. The pine forest might have kept Ella mostly dry if the rain had not been so complete and fierce. Ella rested on the ground for a long time, soon becoming drenched from her long hair to her worn out heart to her tattered shoes.

Tanner was beside himself as he watched the flames roar and the smoke ascend. He tried to get past the thicket but was not able. The luminescent tree caught his eye, and he stopped for a moment in amazement. Then he followed in its direction but got lost once again.

He remained lost until he heard a sound that might have been Ella.

It was dark by the time Ella awoke. Her insides still felt filled with smoke, and she had difficulty breathing. She sat up and coughed loudly.

Tanner was not far and ran toward the noise.

"Ella? Ella, is that you?" He could not make out her figure in the darkness.

"Tanner?"

He knelt by her side and began feeling her face and shoulders and arms. "Are you all right? Are you burned? Are you hurt?"

Ella sat up as far as she could. "Tanner, did you see it? Did you see the tree?"

"Yes, I saw it." His voice became excited. "It was your tree, Ella. It must have been. It was beautiful."

Ella continued to cough.

"We should get you back to the kingdom castle. There are men there who know cures and medicines."

Ella's voice was solemn. "I can't go back to the castle. There is nowhere that I can go."

They were both quiet now. Ella was desolate, and Tanner did not know how to comfort her. Ella did not want to talk about what had just happened, the prince or castle, or her family. Instead, she thought of something amusing to say. "I knew that if you came to rescue me . . . you would certainly be late."

Tanner tried to look into her eyes. The rain was beginning to slow into a trickle, but not before much of Tanner's clothes were damp. He tucked a piece of Ella's wet hair behind her ear. "I think that I might kiss you to keep your lips busy with something other than insulting me."

For a moment those words were all she thought about. Would he really kiss her? She hid her face from him while she spoke. "If you think you can do it without getting lost."

That was one challenge that Tanner would not fail at, and kissing was the one thing he was not clumsy about.

Ella coughed her way out of the kiss. "I believe you have just sucked the last air out of my lungs, and now I surely must die."

She was only joking, but Tanner did not think it was funny. "We need to get you back. I will go and find Cassandra . . ."

"Please don't leave me alone here. I've been alone for too long. I'm too weary to travel. Please just lie beside me and keep me warm. Besides, if you go to find Cassandra, you will most likely get lost."

Tanner kissed her lips for a second time until she again began to cough.

"I don't want to see her anyway. She abandoned me." Ella coughed through her words.

Tanner was determined. "We will not make it back to the castle as fast without her."

"I can't go to the castle!" She used too much strength to say it.

"You can and you must."

"I don't want to go to the castle." Ella's voice was getting weaker, but she was growing impatient.

"Shhh. Don't talk anymore. Let me at least get you to some shelter for the night. Then I will go and find Cassandra. You will surely get worse if you stay in those clothes. I will bring you back a blanket."

Ella couldn't bear the thought of being left alone, but she tried to be brave. "Promise you won't go and get lost?"

Tanner reached his arms down to lift her up. "I promise."

Tanner carried Ella and, with her help, found the inn she had already used on her expedition.

He set her down on the same bed she had rested in before, where she curled up and began to shiver. "Try to get some rest. I will be back shortly." He watched with worry for another moment as she wrapped her arms as tightly around her legs as she could.

"It's so cold," Ella whispered with her eyes closed.

Perhaps Tanner had a better sense of direction knowing that Ella was so unwell. He found the horse easily once he had made his way through the heavy brush.

"Cassandra! Cassandra!" He let out a loud whistle, which shot through the pines and returned as an echo. The horse's whinnies also came back to his ears, and he ran in her direction. This time, Tanner forced her through the thorny wood. His shirt was streaked with blood by the time he reached the clearing and the twin pine trees again. He had fought with the horse the whole way and was breathless when he reached Ella. She was still and appeared to be asleep.

"Here is a blanket, Ella."

Ella did not respond. Tanner shook her lightly and she jolted awake with a loud gasp for air.

"Shhhhh. It is only I. Here is a blanket. You must remove your wet clothing."

The bashful knight held the blanket out for her. Ella sat up, and once she had taken the dark wool blanket, her knight left her alone while she carefully slipped out of her wet clothing and wrapped the blanket tightly around herself. The familiar blanket brought her comfort. It was the same one she had used while traveling with the knight and the prince's aides. It had been the only thing to comfort her then as well. Ella chose a different bed this time, as the one she had rested in before was now soaking wet. She wished the bed was more like a hole that she could crawl inside to escape and hide from the whole world. She was almost asleep when Tanner knocked at the door. He entered after waiting for an answer and only hearing silence.

"Ella?" He could not see her and became frantic. "Ella?"

Loud coughs that sounded inhuman sent Tanner in a rush until he lowered himself in front of her.

"Oh, Ella. You sound as though you are at death's door. Please let me take you back to the castle tonight."

"I cannot think of going anywhere tonight. Please don't mention it again. I will make it through."

The knight bowed his head in defeat. "Would it be wrong of me to ask if I may stay in the same room with you tonight?"

"I don't mind." Ella's voice was hoarse and weak, and every time she spoke she broke into a cough.

Tanner walked to the other side of the room and lay down on a bed opposite hers so that he could face her. He stayed up most of the night, listening in agony to her shallow breaths. But in time, he too drifted.

28

The darkness shattered into pieces as a bright sun rose the next morning. Tanner had slept poorly but was glad to see Ella's face once again in the light of day. The air was cool, but the sun was already warming the earth. Tanner sat up and watched Ella sleep. She was not struggling for breath the way she had the night before, but she looked pale.

"Ella? It's morning, Ella. Wake up. We should get going soon."

Ella did not make any movements or sounds. Tanner quickly retrieved the maiden's clothing from the window ledge.

"Ella, wake up."

Ella began to stir. Tanner set her clothing (which was mostly dry) beside her.

"I'll wait while you get dressed."

Ella moaned. She was not altogether conscious, but she rose once Tanner had left the room. She dressed with immense difficulty, and Tanner did not have to knock on the door because he entered as soon as he heard her body thud on the ground.

Tanner ran to her and shook her arm. It slumped down in front of her. She rolled onto her back, and her entire body was limp.

"Ella! Ella!"

Tanner felt her heart for a beat, and it was thumping faintly. He wrapped the blanket around Ella again for extra warmth, then lifted her up and carried her to the horse.

Cassandra could sense that something was wrong. She was eager to be untied again and began anxiously moving her legs.

"Be still, girl. Hold steady while I lift her up."

He wrapped Ella's arms around Cassandra's neck and tried to hold her in place while he lifted himself up. Her body rested on top of Tanner's arms and the horse's mane as they rode swiftly through the forest.

The slowest part of their ride was through the thorny thicket once more, although Cassandra seemed less frightened by it this time. Once they were out of it, she moved with force and precision up the mountainside and through the woods. She seemed to know that she was headed for the castle and that a stable and plenty of food and water would be waiting.

Tanner's resolve got them to the castle before evening. He rode straight to the front entrance and carefully slid off the creature. A gentle pull on Ella was all it took for her to fall gracefully into his arms. He whispered in her ear. "It seems I am only clumsy when you are awake to see it." He kissed her cheek before beginning a swift walk to the castle door.

"Please," he begged the guard. "Please let us in. She needs to see a medicine man."

The red-headed guard was unsympathetic. "Tanner, you escaped prison. I have no choice but to put you back into the prison dungeons." Two armored knights began walking toward them, their hands on their swords.

"I don't care what you do with me . . . after I take her to the sick chambers."

"Tanner, I cannot help you. It is my neck if I do so!"

Tanner lowered his head in frustration and sighed. A single tear slipped from his eye. The guard took notice.

"I really cannot let you in, Tanner. It would be bad for you . . . and me . . . and maybe even the girl.

I know of a medicine man that lives in Oakwood. It is not far from here. You may even reach him by sundown. We have been given specific orders that if we see either one of you we are to throw you into the prison dungeons. You are not welcome at the kingdom castle. If you really want to help her, take her to Oakwood. That is all I can do for you." He held out his hands to the knights who were still ready to draw their swords. "Stand down, men."

Tanner moved his legs as fast as he could under the weight of Ella's slumping body. He found Cassandra just outside the gate and propped Ella up once more on the horse's back.

They rode as quickly as possible. Cassandra was not as willing because she had not had enough to eat. But they managed to reach Oakwood before sundown.

Tanner rode the horse into the center of town. The village square was still bustling, but he could see that many were beginning to move away from it, probably toward their homes. He asked everyone he saw if they knew of a medicine man. After a while, Tanner began to think that the guard had been lying, or maybe even setting a trap. Then in the sky he saw a strange yellow-colored smoke rising from the forest. He decided to find its source.

A round cottage with a peaked roof stood a distance from the village square. The smoke was coming from behind the cottage. Tanner steered Cassandra around the building, where they found a man hunched over a fire, throwing in some yellow-hued plants. He wore a robe of black and red and was obviously from another country, given his dark skin and small frame. He was much shorter than Ella, let alone any of the men in the kingdom. He would probably only come to Tanner's chest.

"Excuse me, sir!" Tanner called. "Do you know of any medicine men that live here in Oakwood?"

"I only know of one," the man said in his foreign accent as he continued throwing the fluffy plants into the moderate flames.

Tanner watched him curiously and impatiently. "Do you know where I might find him, sir?" It added to Tanner's annoyance that Cassandra kept trying to eat the plants. He pulled back on the reins to stop her.

The man looked at Tanner for the first time and said, "I am he."

"Sir, I need your assistance." Tanner's earnestness and desperation were evident. "There is a girl that needs your help."

The man looked around Tanner. "I do not see a girl. I only see you." He went back to his burning.

"She is here, sir. Resting on the horse."

The man looked closer. "Ah, yes. I thought perhaps that you had four legs, but now I see the girl. You had better bring her inside." He walked toward the house. "Tie your horse up and I will prepare a bed for her."

The man's house was dotted with trinkets. They were on shelves, tables, stools, and the floor against every wall. A large dog sat by the indoor fire. The man poked at the flames for a moment, his bald head sweating in front of the heat. Tanner kicked the door and entered with Ella in his arms.

"Bring her to me," the man said.

Tanner laid her down on the low bed. Her complexion was finally beginning to redden from being in the overheated room. The man looked her over.

"You two would make a fine match," the man said, like it was his only discovery so far.

"Perhaps someday, sir," Tanner said. At the moment, Tanner was only concerned with Ella's well-being, even if the idea was something that had crossed his mind more than once. "Things are a little complicated right now."

The man looked at Tanner. "There's no time like the present."

"Perhaps I should at least wait until the girl is awake."

"Perhaps," the man said. "What is her name?"

"Ella. Ella of Willow Top. She was caught in a fire and inhaled a lot of smoke, sir. She was having trouble breathing when she went to sleep last night. She was soaked from the rain when I found her, and would not wake up after fainting this morning."

The man worked in silence, feeling around her head and neck, placing his ear to her chest to listen to her breathing, examining her limbs for injury. Much of her arms and legs were covered with cuts.

After a while he paused and looked as though he was in deep reflection.

Tanner cleared his throat to try to get the man's attention.

"I do not think it is the smoke," he said slowly while he began to examine her once more.

"What is it then?"

He stopped again to look at Tanner. "I believe it is her tree."

"Her tree?" Was it really possible that all of her current sickness was because of her tree?

"Something has happened to her tree. Does she have any enemies?"

"A fair few by now, I'd guess."

"She is dwindling, but she still has time. Do you think you can find her tree?"

Tanner thought of the image he had seen of the floating tree. "It was a fruit tree. It must be in the kingdom orchards. That is quite close to the castle."

The man nodded in understanding. "I will look after the girl. You must go and help her tree."

"Thank you . . . um . . ."

"Crane. You may call me Mr. Crane." He placed his palms together and bowed toward Tanner.

Tanner accepted his bow and ran out the door. He was glad that he knew a sure way to the castle from Oakwood. He could find it easily, even in the dark.

29

It was late when Tanner passed the castle. Only a few lights shone in the windows and towers. The kingdom orchards were not even a mile from the castle, and Cassandra made the trek easily, despite having been underfed recently.

Tanner tied Cassandra up at the gated entrance of the orchard. It was much too dark. He could not even tell which type of tree was which as he walked through the rows. The moon's light was absent.

Yet he could not stop looking. There had to be some way to find her tree, even in the darkness. Tanner combed the rows looking for anything out of the ordinary. And then he saw it: a slumping apple tree hedged in by the same type of thorny brush that surrounded the prince's tree. They were crawling up the trunk, and Tanner only had to watch for a moment to see that the thicket suffocating Ella's tree was getting bigger and stronger. Frantic, he began looking around him for help. He even pulled at the thicket with his bare hands, which got him nothing but a slice across the whole of his left palm. Dark, wet blood began to ooze.

Tanner quickly ripped a cloth from his shirt and tied it tightly around his hand. Then he began running to the other end of the orchard where he knew a shed filled with gardening tools stood.

A few clouds parted, allowing the moon to show a bit of her light. Tanner made his way back to the tree with an ax and a shovel. Despite its slumping, he recognized Ella's tree, with its broad span and fullness. Many of the leaves had fallen to the ground. Much of the fruit as well, but there was still life clinging onto every branch.

Tanner walked around it once and then began hacking with the ax. It wasn't long before much of the thicket was off of Ella's tree.

The shovel was next. The roots of the bushes were shallow and thin; digging them out was easier than Tanner had thought it would be. But they were so entangled, and there were so many, that the faithful knight dug for the rest of the night, not knowing if any of his efforts were helping Ella at all.

Whenever he loosed a portion of the thicket, he carried it outside the perimeter of the orchard and placed it in a pile. Often, when he returned to her tree, there were new shoots already beginning to wind around the others, which caused him to work even faster. By daybreak, the pile was heaping so much that he had to start another. Tanner was exhausted, and to make things worse, he could see a line of gardeners and servants walking from the castle straight toward the orchard.

Digging in the dark had been difficult, but it would be impossible during the day while people walked about the fruit trees. Someone might see him, and pleading with gardeners would be pointless, especially if someone recognized him. He didn't belong there, and somebody would certainly protest his presence. All he could do now was hope that some of the gardeners would see Ella's tree and try to take care of it.

Tanner put the tools back where he had found them and hid at the back side of the shed, which bordered a large wheat field and would make an excellent hiding place. He let Cassandra go free, and she trotted off to the stables, surely to find something to fill her belly with.

Knowing that there wasn't much else he could do at the time and feeling as though his eyes were double in size, he lay down behind the orchard and tried to get some sleep.

When the gardeners returned to the shed at the end of the day, the sounds of voices speaking and metal clanking pulled Tanner from a deep sleep. He jerked up. The sun was getting low, but once they were all gone, he would still have a little bit of daylight to work with.

It didn't take the men and women long to clean up the tools and head back for the castle.

Tanner retrieved a shovel and ax once again and ran to Ella's tree.

It appeared as though the gardeners had not worked in the orchard that day. All of his efforts had been in vain; the tree looked as grown over and droopy as it had in the night. The piles of dug-out thickets he had made were still standing just outside the orchard. New brush was growing all the time around Ella's tree.

That would not deter him. Tanner wiped his brow and picked up the ax. Little did he know, someone was watching.

30

Prince Monticello had a scope that was much like the king's, only the prince's scope did not see as far. Sometimes he used the scope to spy on his aides or his band of soul catchers to make sure they were doing as they had been instructed. But once in a while, he looked over the portion of the kingdom his scope would allow him to see out of sheer boredom. He would set it up in his tower and watch for some struggling soul so that he could have a laugh, as it was his sick pleasure to see people suffer.

This is what he was doing as he waited for the clock to move to the time of the ball, and soon he saw one of his knights digging up the thickets that he had planted the day before. He immediately called for one of his aides to prepare a horse, armor, and sword for a last-minute matter of business.

Cinder had mixed feelings as she got dressed for the ball. The thought of being with the prince excited her, but she still felt as though she had betrayed her sister by trusting him. She didn't know who to believe and thought it was only right to get to know the prince better.

She had borrowed one of Katrina's new dresses this time. It was a dark, dark blue and nowhere near as plain as her last one had been. One of the servants spent a good deal of time working on Cinder's silver hair. She was nothing short of breathtaking with the dark blue against her light skin and with her hair pulled up away from her face. The servants helping her fawned over her until Cinder blushed, which added a lovely hue of red to her cheeks. Cinder smiled at herself in the mirror, pleased with the final look.

When she was ready, Cinder nervously paced her small room until it was time to go. She asked the servants to leave her alone for a moment. The door closed behind them, and Cinder looked in the mirror. Never would she have imagined herself looking the way she did that night, and she was very pleased.

The corridors got busier with life as she moved farther from the servants' quarters and closer to the ballroom. Her head popped into the room, and she looked for nobody but the prince. He was not seated at the grand table or anywhere. The people that were the most familiar were William and Flesher. Luckily, William did not notice her. Flesher made eye contact with her and began to motion an invitation for her to come into the room. Cinder pulled herself out of the doorway and leaned against the wall.

The prince's face was the only thing she wanted to see, the only thing that she had been looking for as her eyes moved up and down the grand hall, and the only thing that would have made her feel at all like she belonged in the room with all of those grand people.

Ella's tree seemed to be improving little by little. Darkness was beginning to take over the light, and Tanner was in a hurry to get as much done as he could before the light was gone completely. His shovel beat repeatedly into the ground under the roots of the black underbrush when a horse came up behind him and a voice stopped his every movement.

"What exactly do you think you are doing?"

Cinder waited for over an hour. If she was honest about how she felt, she would say she felt foolish. Just as she was about to leave, a hand grabbed her arm to pull her toward the ballroom.

"Don't go. I was hoping you would come in and dance with me. Are you waiting for someone?" Flesher was admiring her as he spoke.

"Um . . . I was waiting for the prince, but . . ." Cinder began looking around again.

"The prince had somewhere to go tonight. Did he not tell you?"

"No," Cinder said. Her faith in the prince was beginning to dwindle.

"Well, I would love to have you come in and dance. You may sit by me. You look stunning tonight, Cinder."

Cinder would have been flattered by his words if she was not so disturbed by the news about the prince. Surely he could have sent word to her that he would not be able to come if he cared for her at all, even if his flight was important. "I don't think so. I am suddenly not feeling very well." Cinder bowed her head and fidgeted with her fingers.

"Is there anything I can do to help you?" His voice was filled with true concern, but Cinder did not notice.

"No, thank you." She was in a great hurry to be away from the whole experience. "I can manage."

She left him bewildered and standing alone as she walked away from the grand ballroom. The servants' quarters and her own room were not her destination. Fresh air and sky called to her from outside, and she found the closest exit to try to escape the strange way she was feeling. Her feet stepped onto a path outside the castle wall, behind the back gardens, and she was on her way to one of her favorite places at the kingdom castle: the orchard.

31

Tanner was not afraid of the prince. He was not concerned about a sword fight or about his own possible death or imprisonment. Ella was his only concern now. He feared that now that he had been caught, the prince would do whatever it took to destroy Ella's tree quickly and for good.

"A little late-night gardening?" The prince stood with his arms folded.

"You know why I'm here. We do not need to play games like children." Tanner continued to work, watching the prince from the corner of his eye.

"Maybe we do not need to play games, but I do enjoy a little fun."

Tanner stopped and turned his whole body to face the prince. "Is that what you call destroying the life of someone as beautiful as Ella—fun?"

"Well, it would have been more fun if I could have actually seen her die."

"Ella is not dead." He spoke it with conviction.

"She will be," the prince said, his confidence showing in the look of his eyes and in the nod of his head.

The knight slowly drew his sword. The prince drew his own with a smile.

"You know that you cannot win. There is nothing that you can do to hurt me."

"Then I will fight you until you give in."

Prince Monticello let out a single huff of laughter and then began swinging his sword. Tanner stopped each blow with precision but was unable to make any jabs at the prince. The prince flashed his sword through the night sky, and Tanner firmly resisted. Tanner landed on his knee during one of the blows but rose quickly to cut a slice out of the air. The prince backed away momentarily, and their positions switched. Tanner was on the offensive now, inching the prince into a backward dance.

Tanner and the prince made a good sword fighting pair. One's skills and technique were not above the other, and they fought patiently, each waiting for the other to make a wrong move. Every once in a while the prince would swing and hit Ella's tree to ignite the knight. He was never disappointed by this effort. Tanner would increase in speed and force whenever Monticello did this until they both came back down to a comfortable level.

The sounds of spirited, clashing swords reached Cinder's ears as she approached the orchard. She sped up slightly but stayed hidden behind the trees so as not to be seen by the swordsmen.

Cinder lowered herself behind an aged cherry tree and tried to focus her sight on the two fighting men to determine who they were. She recognized the prince immediately and was even more upset that he had ignored her to come out and play at sword fighting. It didn't take long for her to realize, however, that they were not playing. In time, she also recognized Tanner as the man she had been in prison with. She was amazed that he fought the prince with so much passion and thought that he must certainly have a wish to die. She was somewhat disinterested in the fight and the reasons for it until the two men stopped huffing and grunting long enough to exchange words.

"You will never get away with this! The king will stop you!"

"The king!" Prince Monticello laughed. "The king sits in the top of his tower doing nothing. He uses his aides and advisors to run his kingdom and cares nothing for his people—not one. He will certainly not stop me." The prince was out of breath. The blades of the two men locked as they spoke.

"You will not be able to kill Ella until you have first killed me."

"Let's get on with it then," the prince said playfully as he pulled his sword back and began fighting with greater persistence.

Cinder did not know how Ella and Tanner were connected. She did not know what the prince might want with her sister. The only thing she knew in that moment was that her feet could run with great speed, even in a long dress and uncomfortable shoes.

The prince was beginning to take over the sword fight. Tanner felt it and retreated. His fear and falling back forced him to lose confidence, and the prince flung Tanner's weapon away from him. The prince did not waste any time or spout any last-minute words. He simply swung his sword through the air in the direction of the knight's neck when a voice called out to him and a body came in between him and his target.

Cinder had not really meant to stop the prince's blade. Her anger had caused her to run with such speed, and her confusion had prevented her from stopping, so that the prince's sword slashed through her middle. She fell to her knees.

The prince pulled out a cloth and wiped his sword without a second thought.

Cinder held onto her stomach as blood trickled onto her hand and down her dress.

"You should have stayed at the ball, Cinder. Even if your companion was not there to dance with you." He smiled as he spoke.

Cinder's shocked face and mouth spouted gasps and spasms. Tanner stood up and caught her before she fell all the way to the ground.

"It looks like you have enough to keep you busy for now. I will leave you alone to choose whether to save the girl you love or her sister."

Prince Monticello ambled to his horse, mounted, and, without looking back, rode toward the castle.

Tanner truly was torn. As he sat with the dying girl, he watched Ella's tree begin to shrivel and dry up once again. The thorny shrubs he had worked so hard to clear out began to strengthen and multiply before his eyes. He imagined Ella lying in the house of a strange man, and it was as if he could see her beginning to suffocate once again. His clothes and hands were stained with Cinder's warm, wet blood. He closed his eyes and hoped for help.

The prince entered the kingdom castle and beheld a face that he hadn't seen in a long time. The face stared back with anger and judgment, and all of the prince's confidence seeped from his countenance.

"You have done enough here, Monticello." The king's voice was low, and while it was not loud, it was full and piercing.

"Exactly what are you going to do? I see that you have come down from your tower to pay a visit to your lowly subjects." The prince began to circle the king, acting with coolness, as though he was unaffected, when really he was quivering on the inside. "What do you think of my work here tonight?"

"I think it is enough to have you banished. You no longer have a place in this castle. Nor do you have access to any aides or advisors, unless of course they are willing to leave the castle with you."

Prince Monticello fumed. He stood up on his toes to get directly in the king's face. "You cannot banish me, old man! You cannot touch me!"

The king reached out a finger and placed its tip on the prince's forehead. "Touch," he said. He pulled back his finger so that he was pointing at the prince, right between his eyes. "You cannot take back the things that you have done and you are not fit to be king. You will never have my throne. And while you cannot die from the point of a kitchen knife, and your tree cannot be chopped, burned, or dug out, you seem to be forgetting that my power exceeds yours and always will."

Prince Monticello was sweating and shaking with rage, but his words were still clear as he spoke between clenched teeth. "If you make me leave this castle, there will be no end to the destruction that I will cause."

The king spoke with perfect mildness. "Then let me remind you of something: You only have power as it is given to you by others. And every time you are defeated, you lose some of that power. Ella will survive. And her roots will be so deep that you will never again be able to hurt her. And it will be the same with every person who triumphs over you."

The prince stepped back but kept his eyes locked on the king's.

"Leave. You may not take anything with you or speak to anyone. All of your things will be burned."

Monticello did not move, so the king reiterated. "Leave. And do not ever come back. A band of knights will be escorting you from the kingdom."

Four knights entered the hallway from outside after hearing the king's cue. Resignation was the only thing left for the prince to claim. He turned away from his father and walked into the darkness.

32

Cinder coughed weakly and tried to speak. "Is that . . . Ella's tree?"

"Yes," Tanner said. What was he going to do?

"Will you . . . take me . . . to it?" She coughed heavily and held onto her bleeding middle with her soaked right arm.

"No. Let me get you back to the castle. Then I will come back and take care of Ella's tree." Tanner tried to lift Cinder's dipping body onto Cassandra.

"No, Tanner. I can . . . save her. If you . . . lay me down . . . so that . . . my body touches the tree." She had to stop and cough. Blood was coming out of her mouth now. "My life . . . will transfer to her tree. It will save her."

It was true. Tanner had learned it in his training at the castle. If a person was dying, they could lie down next to a dying tree, and the tree would be saved. At least, that was what the legend said. He had never seen it, though, and he wondered if it would really work.

"Please," Cinder said before closing her eyes and giving in to sleep.

He was almost willing to try it. But he still had hope that it was possible to save both of them.

Tanner continued to try to get Cinder back onto the horse until he saw a figure speedily approaching them on horseback. He feared it was the prince and glanced around for his sword while still carefully cradling Cinder's body.

The sound of the horse's pounding feet came closer and closer. It was not the prince. "Let me see the girl," a breathless voice said in the darkness. He pulled the horse to a halt and swung down in one graceful, quick motion.

The man was short and wore a cloak about his shoulders. He had long, wavy hair that he brushed away from his face to inspect the body that still rested in the knight's arms.

"Lay her down here," the man said, pointing to an open space.

Tanner was not sure whether he could trust the man or not. Sensing his uneasiness, the man explained who he was. "My name is Lord Barton. I am one of the king's men skilled in medicine. He has sent me to help the girl if I can. She looks bad, but I cannot see well enough out here."

Tanner quickly but carefully placed Cinder on the ground and showed the man where the wound was. He watched as Lord Barton dressed her wounds and chanted a song. Then the lord placed herbs on her lips. Tanner began to squirm. Now that Cinder was in capable hands, he wanted to be back at Ella's tree.

"If you would, good knight. Help me get the girl onto the horse and we will take her back to the kingdom castle." Lord Barton and Tanner lifted Cinder from the ground onto the lord's horse. The medicine man sat behind Cinder, trying to cradle and protect her body while Tanner led the horse at a medium pace back to the castle.

Once Cinder was taken into a dimly lit room inside the castle, Lord Barton thanked Tanner and gave him permission to leave. "I'll do my best to help her."

Tanner ran outside and mounted the same horse he and Lord Barton had just used to carry Cinder back to the castle. The saddle and horse were wet from Cinder's blood, as was Tanner. Under the knight's firm kick, the horse raced back to the orchard and straight to Ella's tree. Tanner leaped off and reached for the ax that was still on the ground.

The thorny shrubs were now crawling toward the tips of each branch. So much so that it was hard to see the tree beneath them at all. The moon was high in the sky, but it was little help to Tanner given the sliver that it was.

None of this deterred the faithful knight. With the anger he felt toward the prince, his gratitude for the king and the medicine man that he had sent, and his love for Ella, Tanner worked through the night with vigor, digging, swinging the ax, and trying desperately to save the only thing he loved.

33

The sun rose bright and hot, but it was nothing to the light and heat blazing from the heaps of shrubbery that Tanner had piled up and lit. With the help of a few other knights, whom the king had sent in the night, the tangled shrubs had been moved away from the orchard to a spot where they would burn safely and quickly. Once the dark trees had been dug up, it did not take long for them to die. As the first smoke began to rise, Tanner raced to the stables to find a horse.

A dark brown steed was in the first stall and, not wanting to waste any time, Tanner pulled him out of the stables and mounted without worrying about a saddle or even whom the horse belonged to.

He rode with great trepidation, fearing that Ella had slipped from this world before he had been able to clear out all of the thorny branches that had been suffocating her tree. While all of the damaging brush was gone, the brittle branches on Ella's tree still hung toward the ground.

When Tanner forcefully entered the home of Mr. Crane, Ella's smile calmed all of his anxiety. She was sitting in the bed, and Mr. Crane was feeding her soup from a spoon.

"Ah, Sir Tanner. Welcome. You are just in time. This is the best-tasting chicken that I have ever had the privilege of head-chopping."

The kind medicine man's smile and words were also helpful in lifting the knight's spirits. Tanner could not eat, however, until after telling Ella what had happened to her sister. He relayed all of the events of the day before and then apologized for having been in such a hurry to return to her that he had forgotten to check on Cinder before he left.

"My poor sister." Ella sighed heavily. "But she is receiving medical care?"

"Yes, very good care, I believe."

"Let us be grateful then that you were able to find your way without getting lost." Ella smiled a small, devious smile and then became serious again. "Will you take me to her?"

Tanner was usually quick to answer, but he paused reflectively. "You know that I would take you anywhere that you asked. But before I answer, I have something to ask of you. Ella of Willow Top, will you be my wife?" The knight moved to kneel down as he proposed, and as he did, he slipped forward and spilled the bowl of hot soup all over the maiden that he was proposing to.

"Well, I might have said yes," Ella answered as she waited for Mr. Crane, who was scrambling for a cloth to dry her.

"Don't worry, Tanner. I know how to treat a good burn," said Mr. Crane as he handed the cloth to Ella.

His words were no longer comforting to the humiliated knight. Nor was Ella's chanting of "It's hot, hot, hot."

Ella noticed his misery and moved a hand to his face.

"I will still say yes," she whispered.

"Really?"

"I would be a fool to turn down your proposal, my good knight . . . no matter how clumsy you are."

"I am also a magistrate," hinted Mr. Crane.

"With all due respect, sir, I believe I would at least like to be wearing something dry when I get married." Ella smiled at the man who had taken such good care of her, then looked to Tanner and became somber. "Is she bad?"

"She was bad when I last saw her. We should be off."

"Ella is well enough to travel," said the kind medicine man. "She should also get stronger each day and make a full recovery."

"I don't know how to thank you, Mr. Crane," Tanner said as he shook the man's hands.

"You may come back someday and mop my floor." All of his crooked teeth showed through his smile.

"Thank you," Ella said with fondness and admiration.

Tanner went to lift Ella, but Ella begged to walk since she had been down for so long.

"Where's Cassandra?" Ella asked as she beheld the dark brown steed with large, captivating brown eyes that waited patiently for his riders.

"No idea." Tanner began untying the gentle horse.

"You need to get a different horse," Ella suggested.

"I agree." Tanner helped Ella onto the horse, who immediately took a liking to her. The feeling was mutual.

They rode quickly back to the castle. As they approached the wall and gate, Tanner remembered his greeting the last time he had come to the castle. He asked Ella to wait outside while he tried to gain admittance.

The guard told Tanner about how the prince had been thrown out of the castle and that they were now welcome to come inside by the allowance of the king. Tanner went back for Ella.

"He's gone, Ella," Tanner told her. He grabbed her by the hands and pulled her toward the castle.

"Who's gone?"

Tanner was walking fast now, and Ella was struggling to keep up. "The prince."

Ella stopped, and Tanner followed suit once he realized he was leaving her behind. He turned around to face her.

"What does that mean?" Ella asked. "Is my father now recovered as well?"

Tanner did not know the answer. "Let's go and see how Cinder is. Then we will find out about your father."

They found their way to the sick quarters. Cinder was not as well as they had hoped. Upon seeing her sister, Cinder tried to speak. "Oh, Ella. I am so sorry."

"Shhhhh. Do not speak, Cinder. You do not need to apologize for anything. You need only rest now and try to get yourself better."

"I should have listened to you." Cinder began coughing, and Lord Barton walked over to them all. He tried to ignore their conversation while attempting to make Cinder more comfortable.

"Yes, you should have," Ella agreed. "But we cannot change what has happened. Maybe it was all for the better. The prince is gone now. The only thing I want you to think about is getting well." Ella watched Cinder's dark eyes. They stood out with how pale her face was. "There is nothing you could do to change my love for you, dear sister." Ella sat on the bed beside her sister and kissed her forehead.

"She is improving," Lord Barton said softly. "But she may never return to her full strength again.

Ella gripped Cinder's hand and gave it a soft squeeze. "Hold on, Cinder. Hold on."

34

Tanner once again took up his duties as a knight in the kingdom castle, and Ella sat by her sister day after day, helping her to overcome the wounds that the prince had left her with. Some were physical and would scar. Others were not and would be left as they were, with Cinder able to return to them again and again and feel the pain afresh.

After a few weeks, when autumn was peaking and the whole kingdom seemed to change colors, Flesher began visiting Cinder daily, and Ella never failed to remind him that he had once been her kidnapper.

Ella watched as Cinder's apprehension and mistrust toward Flesher turned to fondness, and when Ella felt comfortable enough to leave them alone, she ventured to the tower above what had once been the prince's chambers. There, in the center of the crescent, sat her father, unchanged, seemingly unmoved. Ella tried to speak to him, but his reactions were the same as when she had come with the prince before.

When Cinder was well enough to walk, Ella took her to see their father.

"I can't imagine what he is going through," Ella said as the two sisters stood over their father.

Tears slipped down Cinder's face. "It hurts me greatly to see him." Cinder dabbed her eyes with a cloth. "The king came to see me—before you and Tanner returned. I asked him about Father. He told me that he doesn't feel much of anything. That giving in to the powers of the prince brings mostly numbness." Cinder looked at her sister. "I will watch over him, Ella. I can take care of him while I work here at the castle."

"That brings me comfort, Cinder. You'll never know how much." Ella hooked arms with her sister.

The two walked the corridors of the kingdom castle daily as Cinder got stronger and stronger. It was as Lord Barton had said, though. She would never regain her full strength and youth.

"What of the others?" Cinder asked Ella one day.

"What do you mean?" They always walked arm in arm, Ella supporting Cinder.

"Mother, Katrina, and Beatrice. Who will look after them?"

Ella hadn't thought much about them, having been so concerned for Cinder. But it was time to make plans for them, or at least plans that included them. "I will take Beatrice to live with Tanner and me when we have found a place to settle."

"What about Katrina?" Cinder asked. Their walk had slowed as they spoke until they finally stopped.

"Katrina is old enough. She does not need anybody to take responsibility for her. What she needs is to be forced to take responsibility for herself."

Cinder laughed. "You have not changed, Ella."

"Nor have you. You are still as good and kind as you always were." Ella looked into her sister's eyes and smoothed a few strands of her silver hair.

Cinder smiled. "I will invite Katrina to live with me at the castle. Oh, can you picture the look on her face?"

"Have it your way. But I don't think that would be good for her character."

Cinder became solemn. "That will leave mother alone." She watched Ella's face become sober as well. "Ella, with everyone gone, and with Katrina and myself so far away, you will have to look after mother."

Tears built up in Ella's eyes until they were full, but she held them back. "But mother has forgotten me."

"Oh, Ella. Mother has not forgotten you. Don't you see? Mother welded us together, so that we could be one. Is it such a bad thing to be a part of me? I do not mind being a part of you."

Ella pondered her words for a time, and then they began to stroll again.

"Do not give up on her, Ella. Or father."

35

Ella and Tanner were married at the castle, and once the ceremony was over, Ella was summoned by the king for a private audience.

Ella waited in the great circular room that she had been in only once before. It felt so peaceful and quiet that Ella had trouble imagining how life was being carried on below them and throughout the kingdom. If only everyone could learn to sit and be as quiet as the king and queen seemed to be.

The king entered and embraced Ella as he had once before. He held her tight for several seconds and then pulled away and motioned with his hand to the lounge. "Sit with me, Ella."

They sat down on the lounge, which was the color of creamy, fresh milk with shining gold swirls. The king looked searchingly into Ella's eyes. "The prince has been sent from the kingdom castle. I think he left knowing that you would never give up on destroying him."

"Why didn't he kill me?"

"He tried. I told you before that the prince had certain powers. But he will never be as powerful as you and your sister. Darkness brings a different kind of power, one that will dim and fade until it is erased altogether. You and your sister are so full of light that with a little help you were able to withstand his attempts. Your trees are strong. And I was always keeping watch."

Ella looked down at her hands that rested palm-up in her lap. "But how is it that you have allowed him to carry on for so long? Why have you only now thrown him out and not before?"

The king did not stutter or hesitate. Everything he spoke came out with perfect clarity. "I think for a time I had hoped that he would turn around. And as he got worse, I thought it was better to keep him here so that I could see closely what he was doing and help where possible."

His words were clear, but she still didn't fully understand.

"Do you remember what I told you, Ella? When you came before? Sometimes I interfere, as I did with you and Cinder, and sometimes I trust in those who are being affected to find their way out of his grasp. You had done everything that you could to ward him off, and it still wasn't enough. But most of the people who find themselves entrapped are there because of the choices that they have made." He paused for a moment. "Like your father."

Ella thought about the prince's tree. Her memory concerning it was unclear.

"Why wasn't I able to destroy the prince's tree? It *was* the prince's tree, wasn't it?"

"Yes, Ella. It was. I told you that the prince had a tree, but what I did not tell you was that he is no longer connected to it at all. You may take the tree of somebody evil. You may dig it up, or burn it, or cut it to the ground, and the person will continue to walk along—not living, but not dead either. The prince has played with darkness for so long that his tree is indestructible, just as he is. It is without spirit. It is merely an object. It no longer has the capacity to produce goodness, and therefore it is no longer vulnerable to anything. Even if you could destroy the tree, such an act would not destroy him."

It was still difficult for Ella to understand his words.

Ella looked at the king with pleading eyes. She remembered what he had told her before, that there was still hope for her father, but she needed to be reassured again. Discouragement was something she was becoming used to. "What about my father? Is he doomed to remain as he is forever?"

"That, I cannot answer. I told you once before that he still has the power to change his circumstances. He simply chooses for now not to exercise that power. He is not like the prince, however, in that he is not evil. Your father is under the influence of somebody evil. That means that, while he does not have a strong connection to his tree right now, there is still hope that someday he will return."

Ella thought of Prince Monticello, dark and handsome but evil to the core. "Is the prince gone forever? Can he do no more harm?"

"I'm afraid he is still out there, even if you do not always see him. But I will keep watch, Ella."

"Can anything be done to stop him?" It was overwhelming to Ella to think about the possibility of facing him again.

The king reflected for a moment.

"Plant seeds, my dear. Plant good seeds, and maybe, someday, if there is enough good in the world, we will be able to overcome him." He thought some more. "But evil is not something that is ever totally absent. It is just something you have to choose not to succumb to."

The king and his subject sat in silence for several moments.

"I have something for you, Ella . . . because you and your family have suffered so much. Tanner and Cinder may always remain here for employ at the kingdom castle if they wish. And I have had something prepared for you. A cottage, in Shepherd's Glade, is waiting for you and your husband, even now as we commune."

Ella did not believe what she had heard until she saw that the king was completely serious and was waiting for a reply. A smile formed on her lips, and a few slippery tears of joy found their way down her cheeks. "My dear king, are you sure?"

"Yes," he answered kindly. "I know that you will be happy there."

Ella threw her arms around the king in gratitude and affection. "Thank you," she said, wiping the tears away with her hand.

"There is one thing more. I have sent word to Paul and Fern Robinson of the location of your new home. Fern is waiting anxiously to hear from you herself, and Paul is currently working on a bridge that will make travel between Shepherd's Glade and Riverwood much more efficient."

It was so good to hear those names. Ella smiled, thrilled that she would be able to see them often.

The king held onto her, and his love filled her heart and soul. "Do your best to help your family. They are all counting on you."

"I'll try," Ella promised. "I'll try."

Ella left the quarters of the king and queen to find her knight waiting. They then found Cinder, who had already resumed her duties at the kingdom castle, to say good-bye.

It is difficult to bid farewell to family after a wedding. Ella held her sister tight, thinking of all they had been through together. "I love you, Cinder."

"I love you too. Come and see Father and me often. And take good care of Beatrice."

"I will. And mother too."

Then Cinder whispered into her younger sister's ear, "You are better than you think, Ella. Better than you know."

Ella looked into Cinder's eyes. "If there is any goodness in me, it is because I learned it from you. Good-bye, Cinder."

"Good-bye, Ella." Cinder stroked Ella's cheek, wiping away a stray tear.

Tanner led Ella outside and to the stables. "It turns out that the horse I took to Oakwood was the king's."

Ella thought that might mean that Tanner was in some kind of trouble, but she was wrong.

"He insists that you have it."

Ella stroked the horse's long, broad nose. "He seems more faithful than Cassandra. He is more like you," Ella said to her knight.

"In that case, maybe we should request another. He may end up trying to kill you accidentally."

Ella smiled as she continued to pet the beautiful animal. "Can we call him Weston . . . after my father?"

"Yes, my love. I could never refuse you anything, no matter how simple or grand."

"That is good to know." Ella looked into the eyes of her knight, and this time he was able to kiss her without the fear of her lungs losing too much air.

Epilogue

The couple enjoyed a few weeks alone together in their new home, and then Ella went to get Beatrice before the snows settled in. Ella went during the day, while Tanner was still asleep after his duties at the castle. Katrina had already gone to live with Cinder. The mother sat in her usual place doing her usual thing, and Ella found Beatrice upstairs alone.

"Hello, Beatrice."

Beatrice glanced at Ella but returned her stare to the quilt on which she sat. "Nobody cares for me," she said.

Ella walked quickly to sit beside her troubled little sister. "That's not true." Ella stroked Beatrice's hair to comfort her.

"Everyone has left me here alone. Mother does not even answer when I call anymore."

Ella hugged her sister. "I have come to take you away."

Beatrice released herself from Ella's grip to question her. "Where? Have you found Father?"

Ella looked down and fiddled with some yarn that tied the quilt. "I know where Father is, but I'm afraid he is not coming back. Not now, anyway."

Ella watched her sister's gloom at the sad news.

"Can I see him?" Beatrice asked.

"I do not think that would be a good idea for now, dear one. But perhaps when you are older I will take you to see him."

"Where are we to live?"

"I have married, Beatrice . . . a good knight who works as a castle guard. The king has given us a home in Shepherd's Glade. It is just on the other side of this mountain. We will be able to come and see Mother every day. And we can visit Cinder and Katrina as well."

"I don't want to see Katrina!"

Ella smiled at her sister. She had felt the same way many times. "Maybe not right now, but someday you will. We all need our families, even if at times we think we would rather live without them. And I will take care of you from now on."

Beatrice tried not to smile.

"I am sorry that I was so rotten to you before," Ella said as she pulled gently on a few strands of Beatrice's ratted hair. "Can you ever forgive me?"

The sisters embraced, and the bond they formed in that moment was enough to carry them through all of the rough times they would endure in life. And making Beatrice laugh would be Ella's new point of focus from day to day.

Beatrice cried as she said good-bye to her mother. She tried hugging her, but the mother did not let go of her work and continually tried to see past Beatrice to what she was working on.

Ella comforted her sister by rubbing her shoulder. "I have a horse waiting outside. I would like a moment alone with Mother."

Beatrice wiped her nose with the sleeve of her tattered dress as she walked out of the cottage.

Ella looked down at her mother in pity. "I do not blame you, Mother. I do not blame you for any of it. If you can hear what I am saying, it is I, Ella. I know where Father is, and if you would ever like to go and see him, I will gladly take you. Although, I warn you it is a dreadful sight. Cinder will come and visit when she can, and so will Beatrice and I. I am taking Beatrice home with me. We live in Shepherd's Glade on the other side of the mountain.

I hope that someday you will be able to come and see us. You are always welcome."

Ella kissed her mother on the cheek and, for a moment, the mother stopped spinning. Ella turned to leave, and the woman resumed her endless work.

As they reached the top of the mountain, Ella looked upon the stump of her father's tree. There came a moment on that short ride home, when Ella felt so many opposites at one time—sorrow and joy, hope and despair, love and hate—that she thought her heart might split in two.

But the following spring, when the snows melted and the trees decided to grow again, Ella visited her father's tree once more. And there, out of the stump of the tree that had once been cut down by her eager knight, Ella found . . . a willow sprout.

Book Club Questions

1. When one member of a family is struggling, what effect can it have on the other family members?
2. What things exist today that tear families apart?
3. Even when we live the best that we know how, will our own ends be "happily ever after?" Is there such a thing?
4. Why do you think the mother of the family shut everyone else out?
5. How did going through their struggles together help Cinder and Ella? How are our relationships

strengthened when we struggle together rather than apart?

6. Which character do you identify with more, Cinder or Ella? Or Cassandra?
7. Why do you think the king did not do more to prevent the prince from causing destruction? Do parents sometimes let their children get away with things? Why?
8. If your life was connected to the life of a tree, what kind of tree would it be?
9. How is the commonly known story of Cinderella the same as this book? How is it different?
10. Why do you think that the father still sits in the prince's tower? Are there things that can have that powerful of a hold on us?

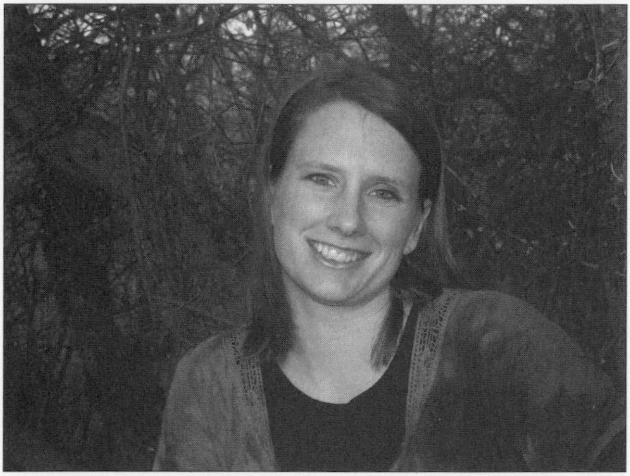

About the Author

Melissa Lemon holds that her greatest achievement is being married to a wonderful man and having three amazing children. In addition to mothering and writing novels, she teaches music lessons on the piano, cello, and guitar. Melissa is a graduate of the University of Utah. She and her family live in Kaysville, Utah.

0 26575 59063 0